James

7 Brides for 7 Brothers
Book 6

ROXANNE ST. CLAIRE

James
7 Brides for 7 Brothers

Copyright © 2016 South Street Publishing
Print ISBN: 978-0-9970627-9-3

This novel is a work of fiction. Any references to historical events, real people, or real locales are used fictitiously. All rights to reproduction of this work are reserved. No part of this publication may be reproduced, stored in or introduced into a retrieval system, or transmitted, in any form, or by any means except for brief quotations embodied in articles or reviews without prior written permission from the copyright owner. For permission or information on foreign, audio, or other rights, contact the author, roxanne@roxannestclaire.com

Published in the United States of America

3 0646 00224 3669

Critical Reviews of Roxanne St. Claire Novels

"St. Claire, as always, brings a scorching tear-up-the-sheets romance combined with a great story: dealing with real issues starring memorable characters in vivid scenes."
— *Romantic Times Magazine*

"Non-stop action, sweet and sexy romance, lively characters, and a celebration of family and forgiveness."
— *Publishers Weekly*

"Plenty of heat, humor, and heart!"
— *USA Today's Happy Ever After blog*

"It's safe to say I will try any novel with St. Claire's name on it."
— *www.smartbitchestrashybooks.com*

"The writing was perfectly on point as always and the pace of the story was flawless. But be forewarned that you will laugh, cry, and sigh with happiness. I sure did."
— *www.harlequinjunkies.com*

"The Barefoot Bay series is an all-around knockout, soul-satisfying read. Roxanne St. Claire writes with warmth and heart and the community she's built at Barefoot Bay is one I want to visit again and again."
— *Mariah Stewart, New York Times bestselling author*

"This book stayed with me long after I put it down."
— *All About Romance*

7 Brides for 7 Brothers

Meet all seven sexy Brannigan Brothers!

1. Luke by Barbara Freethy
2. Gabe by Ruth Cardello
3. Hunter by Melody Anne
4. Knox by Christie Ridgway
5. Max by Lynn Raye Harris
6. James by Roxanne St. Claire
7. Finn by JoAnn Ross

The Barefoot Bay Series

Roxanne St. Claire writes the popular Barefoot Bay series, which is really several connected mini-series all set on one gorgeous island off the Gulf coast of Florida. Every book stands alone, but why stop at one trip to paradise?

The Barefoot Bay Billionaires
Secrets on the Sand
Scandal on the Sand
Seduction on the Sand

The Barefoot Bay Brides
Barefoot in White
Barefoot in Lace
Barefoot in Pearls

Barefoot Bay Undercover
Barefoot Bound (prequel)
Barefoot with a Bodyguard
Barefoot with a Stranger
Barefoot with a Bad Boy

Barefoot Bay Timeless
Barefoot at Sunset
Barefoot at Moonrise
Barefoot at Midnight

Dedication

When my first book was published in 2003, I received a letter from a reader in Italy who informed me I'd made some mistakes on the Italian phrases. She offered to help me if I ever used Italian again. Over the next twelve years, Rossella Re and I became good friends. When I wrote about a series about a large Italian-American family, she was invaluable to me. And when my real-life family and I visited her country last year, Rossella and her awesome husband, Marco, welcomed us into their home and hearts. Getting to know readers is a great part of this job. Becoming lifelong friends with one is a true blessing. This book, set entirely in Italy, is dedicated with all my love to Rossella Re. Of course, she corrected my Italian all the way through. *Grazie mille*, Rossella. *Ti voglio bene, amica mia!*

James

Chapter One

A high-pitched scream of an engine broke through James Brannigan's concentration. He looked up from a stack of documents just in time to see a motor scooter whiz by, so close the bike's handlebar grazed the side-view mirror of the limo taking James up the side of a mountain. His Italian driver chuckled as the Vespa disappeared around the next hairpin turn.

James glanced to the right. That side of the limo was just a millimeter from a knee-high stone wall, the only protection from a thousand-foot drop into the Mediterranean Sea.

Could it be any more complicated, time-consuming, or dangerous to get to Positano, Italy, to visit a winery he'd inherited?

Perhaps Colin Brannigan, when selecting his mysterious "legacies" to give to seven sons upon his death, had mixed James up with one of his younger brothers. Hunter would love nothing more than hanging off that wall by his feet to get the perfect angle for his next *National Geographic* shot. Luke, the fearless documentary producer who lived to trek all over bizarre locales, would salivate at the surroundings. Former Navy SEAL Max could probably climb on top of that wall and shoot someone. Hell, almost any of his six thrill-seeking, speed-demon, danger-loving brothers would love this adventure.

Not James. He wasn't the risk-taker in the family, unless the risk involved money and investments. James needed complete control and, right now, zipping around death-defying turns on the hairy edge of a road that might have been built a few centuries ago…he didn't have any control at all.

Instinctively, he gathered up the papers and refocused on a spreadsheet that didn't quite add up, because work *always* bent to his will. But every time his gaze landed on the column of figures, his mind drifted back to the question that had plagued him all day during this sojourn from New York to Italy.

Why would Colin Brannigan saddle his oldest son with an inheritance that was in every way a massive pain in the ass? James had asked himself that question a hundred times since his billionaire media mogul father died without even telling his seven sons he had cancer, let alone why they'd each inherited a bizarre and inexplicable "legacy."

No money. No part of his vast fortune, at least not until the inheritance would be divided among them in five years. Just a single envelope, each containing…something. James got the deed to Villa Pietro, a two-hundred-year-old winery stuck in the hills above the Amalfi Coast that none of the seven Brannigan brothers even knew their father had owned.

Why, Dad? Why?

The surprisingly big hole left in James's heart when Colin Brannigan died eight months earlier had mostly healed, filled with work and the business of following in his money-making father's footsteps. But today, James had more time than usual to miss his dad and ponder the old man's motives. In fact, in the half day James had flown in his private jet from Manhattan to Naples, then the hour in a helicopter to Sorrento, and now the limo ride on a mountain nature intended to be used only by goats, he'd thought of little else.

Why a winery?

He had no interest in wine, or alcohol of any kind, because it dimmed the laser focus required to run a multibillion-dollar hedge fund. James had never shown any great desire to visit Italy, beyond a trip to Rome for business only. And it wasn't like this little country "villa" that grew grapes in the air would be a jewel in James's portfolio. It commanded a decent price, which he'd negotiate higher after he saw it, but there were discrepancies in the documentation that made him wonder just how well it had been run all these years Dad had owned it.

Even with those issues, he had one offer in hand from a viable buyer, a megacorporation called Whitehouse Wineries known for gobbling up small wineries and turning them into production houses for their brand. It was a brilliant strategy from a well-respected company with a decent amount of zeroes at the bottom line.

It should be easy to sign, sell, and seal a deal.

He perused the Whitehouse offer he'd received via William Hayward, a business manager hired exclusively for this winery—*thanks for that expense, Dad*. Hayward had forwarded the contract with a strong suggestion that James sign it and cash the check. James could have done that, but something stopped him. *Something* made him put his life on hold and travel to southern Italy so he could see this winery in person before he handed it over to new ownership.

Something he didn't like or understand.

He took a slow inhale and looked through the windshield, the postcard view of emerald-green mountains draped in olive groves and lemon trees spilling into the impossibly blue Mediterranean lost on him.

By now, the Brannigan brothers had to face the fact that these little envelopes delivered by their Aunt Claire with essentially no other communication were more than just a nice way for Dad to apologize for a lifetime of being a less-than-perfect father. Each gift, so far at least, had been a catalyst for change in the recipient's life.

James shifted on the plush leather. He didn't want to change. Didn't need to change. Didn't *like* change.

And yet...even from the grave, Dad was pulling strings with these so-called legacies, many of which were unwelcome and complicated. Luke had been given a resort Dad owned near Yosemite, and he liked it—or a woman who ran it—so much so that he ended up making it his home base. Gabe got the family ranch in Calabasas, which made sense since Gabe was a real estate guy, but he didn't sell the place. No, he got married and moved *into* the ranch. Knox landed a vintage motorcycle, which had taken him on quite a ride and settled his fun-loving ass down for good. Hunter went on a literal treasure hunt, only to land some weird poem. Oh, and their grandmother's wedding ring, which he then gave to the woman who'd helped him find it.

That left three of them who hadn't dealt with what their envelopes held. Finn got a small Alaskan airline consisting of three planes, but since he'd been deployed flying carrier duty when Dad died, he was only now getting out of the Navy and planning to go claim the airline. James had, naturally, advised him to sell those planes, but when had the youngest Brannigan brother ever listened to anyone?

Only Max's legacy was closest to what James got—a horse farm in Kentucky. Last time they talked, a little more than a month ago, Max was doing the smart thing and trying to sell the place, but he'd run into some complications with the tenant. Surely he'd worked that out by now.

So James knew, deep in his gut, that he wasn't going to walk away from his legacy until he knew what Dad was trying to tell him from the grave. *Then* he would walk away from it.

Until then, he would wrestle with *why*. Were the legacies for fun, profit, or change? Were they supposed to tell the brothers about their often distant, preoccupied, and uncommunicative father? Were they some kind of posthumous character study?

James didn't need to solve the puzzle of Colin Brannigan. His brothers had far more "issues" with their workaholic father, but James was the oldest, and the most like him. When Mom died and left behind seven boys under thirteen, James had easily assumed the role of second parent and had done his level best to maintain some semblance of control in the chaos that was the Calabasas, California, ranch.

With six brothers ranging from age four to ten and the lively but steady Kathleen Brannigan gone far too soon, James had no choice but to take over while Dad worked. And worked. And worked some more.

From the time he was twelve until he left for Stanford, James would give Dad daily reports like a dutiful employee, highlighting school progress, sports victories, and not a few mishaps on ATVs or fights that had gotten out of hand up in the tree house. Dad would approve or recommend reprimands, and his leadership and decision-making skills soaked into James's head, making James every bit the successful executive his father had been.

No, Dad hadn't been exactly "available" as a father, but business had become James and his father's level playing field and the one thing they had completely in common. James sought advice and shared issues with his father about his rapidly growing hedge fund and the dozens of deals, employees, acquisitions, and trades he managed every day. In exchange, Dad had shared his business empire and given James a glimpse into his life. Nothing too personal, though, not with Colin Brannigan.

He'd mourned his father, yes. But he was also pissed as hell that the old bastard hadn't shared with him the fact that he was dying. Or why the hell they had these arcane *problems* to deal with.

Shaking it off, he looked down at the deed for Villa Pietro one more time. With Colin—as with James—business was life. So there must be a damn good *business* reason he'd given the winery to James.

It had to be because he trusted James to get top dollar in a sale of the place Dad had purchased twenty-four years ago and, as far as he could tell, had never even visited again. So it wasn't like the winery held any sentimental value.

A dilapidated white farm truck rumbled around the next corner, taking up way too much of the road, coming at them at a ridiculous speed. James winced as he gauged how close it would come or, more likely, how hard it would hit. But the limo driver smoothly maneuvered to the right, and the only thing that hit them was a lemon bouncing from a crate on the truck bed.

JAMES

"The Americans are always scared," the driver said with a laugh and thick Italian accent.

"I'm not scared," James replied. "I'm stunned that more people don't die."

"Eh, some do," he said with the culturally distinct wave of his hand. "Wait until you see Positano. You risk life when you cross the street."

Great. "I won't be there long."

"You are staying at the Eden Roc?" he asked. "You won't want to leave. You will cry when you see the view."

He would cry if they didn't have good Wi-Fi, since the Barclay bank deal was going down the next day and he had to conference into the meeting.

"I'm here on business," he said, picking up the papers to let the driver know he wasn't a chatty tourist and views didn't impress him.

"Business in Positano?" he asked. "The only business is sun, sand, and limoncello, *Signor* Brannigan."

"Not wine?" James asked.

"Ah, *sì*. It is Italy," the young man said with a wide grin. "Wine is life. You're here to taste?"

"I'm here to"—*sell*—"visit Villa Pietro. It's a small—"

"Pietro?" His whole face lit up, and he barely missed killing a biker who passed at lightning speed. "I live in Montepertuso, one town from the winery. The Sebastiani family are friends. They have run that winery for many gen…gene…"

"Generations," James supplied.

"Yes, yes. Old Giorgio died a few years ago, sadly, but Anamaria is strong, and if you say she is not, she will hit you, or shove a garlic clove down your throat."

The driver laughed again, but James just stared at him, willing him to get the message that this passenger didn't do small talk.

"Now, Lorenzo and his wife, Elena, run everything," he continued, not getting the clue. "But they'll be handing it to Enzo and Filippa. Of course, there's another brother, Antonio, and Sofia. Oh, Sofia's pregnant with a girl!" He grinned like this was earthshaking news. "*Very* pregnant. Might have had it already."

James nodded and looked down at the papers, preferring to bury himself in numbers rather than the gobbledygook Italian names that all blurred together. Those people were Whitehouse Wineries' problem. Whitehouse wanted to fill the place with their American staff and build their presence in Italy. James just wanted the money and to get Villa Pietro off his books for a decent-sized profit.

"You'll meet them all," the driver nattered on. "With Enzo's boys, Nico and Gianni, they should be running that place for many more years to come. Oh, and there's Bruno." He looked skyward. "*Madonna*. Every family has one of those, *sì*?"

"Right." Whatever Bruno was, the Brannigans probably *did* have one of those. With seven boys, there wasn't a type they couldn't claim.

"They are a nice, big family," he said, the Italian thick but the loving sentiment clear. "I went to school with Antonio."

When James didn't answer, the man's voice finally faded, a shadow of disappointment visible in the dark eyes reflected in the rearview mirror.

"Would you like me to take you there first? To Villa Pietro?"

"No," James said, glancing at the agenda his assistant had prepared, breaking his day into the fifteen-minute slots he preferred. He had a late-night call with a financial analyst in Hong Kong that he had to make immediately, since it was nearly eleven there now. And four different conference calls with his office in San Francisco, where it was still the workday. After that, he'd have dinner in the room, do a bit more reading, and finally sleep.

"Are you sure? In about two kilometers, we will reach a road that will take you up to Villa Pietro."

Up? It was higher than this? God help him. "No, thank you. Just get me to the hotel in Positano, please."

"But you must want to stop for lemon *granita*." He pointed to a lookout jammed with tourists, all taking pictures and surrounding a large yellow and white truck selling some kind of Italian lemonade. "The oldest genuine *granita* in the world, only in Positano," the driver added. "And the view is world famous. *Everyone* stops here."

"I'm not everyone," he said, peering past the crowd to see the world-famous view, which was little more than treacherously balanced pastel buildings that looked like they'd roll down the mountain and onto the beach with the next strong wind.

"It's pretty, yes?" the driver asked, his gaze on James instead of the curve in the road.

"Yes." Pretty remote. "The Hotel Eden Roc, *please*."

The driver got the message and continued on in silence, dodging more scooters, passing trucks, and careening past a thousand parked cars on a road not much wider than a bike path.

Miraculously, no one died. The limo driver pulled up to a hotel that was four stories built into the side of the mountain. The rough stone façade was broken up by wrought-iron balconies covered in the same fuchsia flowers that had to be weeds, considering they popped out of every rock and wall.

Leaving the driver to get his bags, James stepped into a quiet, elegant, and understated lobby, grateful his assistant knew to find him exactly the kind of upscale boutique hotel he preferred.

Before he even got to the desk, a man came up on his left and greeted him by name. A woman behind the desk delivered her *buongiornos* with a huge smile. Another young man joined in the welcome, all of them spewing a mix of Italian and broken English at him as they informed him that he had Suite 6, the best in the building.

A bellman guided him in the direction of an elevator just as a woman nearly knocked him over, jumping right into his path.

"James?" She was petite, barely five-four, with a wild mass of long blond hair and the brightest blue eyes he'd ever seen, sparking like gas flames at him. "Um, I mean, Mr. Brannigan. Sorry." She grinned and rolled her eyes as if her faux pas was just part of her charm. "Mr. Brannigan."

An American, he knew instantly, drawing back at the sheer presence of all that...blond brightness. "Yes. James Brannigan. Can I help you?"

"No, no! I'm here to help you." Dimples, two of them, deep and symmetrical, punctuated her sweet pink lips like a couple of exclamation points.

He glanced at the bellman, rooting for the Italian word for *help*. But the young man stepped back, smiling as if James, of course, wanted this particular distraction on the way to his suite.

She extended her hand, and he took it, closing his hand around slender fingers with a surprisingly strong grip. "Kyra Summers, sir, and we are so happy you're here. So, so happy." Her eyes danced as she shook his hand with the fury of someone trying to explode a soda bottle. "Happy," she repeated.

He'd have to remind his assistant to book him somewhere a little less, well, happy. "It's good to be here, Miss…Summers."

God, the name fit her. She was human sunshine and daisies, with a pink and white cotton dress that revealed tanned shoulders and hugged feminine curves on top and spread to a loose, flowing skirt that fell just above her knees. He forced his gaze back to eyes the color of the skies over his California childhood home.

"We're very excited about your visit," she said, a quiver of nerves apparent in her voice. "It feels like we've been waiting forever for…a Brannigan. And now you're here!"

He let out an uncomfortable laugh at her enthusiasm and glanced again at his bellman, wondering if this really was standard at the Eden Roc. "Yes, I'm here," he said, taking a step toward the hall and elevator.

She came right with him. "Did you have a good trip? Was it long? You're right on time, though, so it went well?" She bit her lip and looked up at him, a cross between a puppy and a…bubbly, sunny, dimply Kewpie doll. He'd have to give the welcoming committee props, though. The greeter was gorgeous, if you liked the effervescent type. He didn't.

"It's all good," he assured her. "I'll just, uh, get to my room."

"Of course!" She clapped her hands like this just occurred to her. "Well, that's fine, you get settled and I'll take you when you're ready." She pointed to a settee under a display of ceramic platters on the wall. "I'll be right here. Where I've been…" She let out a chuckle that sounded more like bells than laughter. "For a while, right, Aldo?"

Aldo nodded and grinned. "She has been waiting," he confirmed in accented English. "Very…*speciale* guest."

"So special!" she agreed. "I'll wait until you're ready. Then we'll go!"

"Go…where?" He frowned and glanced around for assistance, vaguely aware of the irony that the only other American in the room was speaking words that didn't make sense. He wasn't going anywhere; it wasn't on his quarterly hour schedule.

"To dinner," she said. "I know it's early, but there's so much to see and do, and dinner will take hours, and you're on a different time now, so this is…" Her words faded as crystal blue eyes searched his. "You don't want to have dinner?" A little sadness softened her voice and did something stupid to his heart.

Why should he care if he crushed this little imp hired by a hotel to make him feel welcome? "I have to work." The four words rolled off his tongue with as much familiarity as his own name.

"I thought you might…I mean…you have to eat and…"

"I have a call with Hong Kong and conferences," he said, but even as the words came out of his mouth, they sounded as wooden as they tasted.

"Oh." The smile faded. The eyes dimmed. The dimples disappeared.

James felt a physical kick in the gut and no small burn of shame for acting like a dick to this woman who was nothing but nice. "But I could have dinner." As his words came out, they surprised both of them.

Sunshine burst forth again, warming him whether he liked it or not. "Oh, wonderful. I'll wait. I'll take you there." She reached out, almost making him flinch at the unexpected jolt when she made contact with his arm.

JAMES

"We're so happy you're finally here, Mr. Brannigan. We've been waiting and waiting for this very day."

No wonder the hotel ranked so high. "Thank you," he said, taking a slow step away. "I should make a call, but…"

But Hong Kong would be there tomorrow. And he was suddenly famished.

"Take your time." She backed away and dropped onto the settee, the pink skirt spreading like flower petals against the silk. "I'll be right here." He must have looked a little stunned at his own decision, because she added a reassuring smile and said, "It'll be fun."

"Fun." He repeated the word, as foreign as the language in this country. James Brannigan didn't do fun. He didn't do impulsive blondes with captivating smiles and too many exclamation points, either.

Well, apparently, he did in Italy. "I'll just be a few moments, Miss Summers."

"Kyra," she corrected. "My name is Kyra."

It sounded as musical as she was, and James was only a little surprised that he was still smiling when he stepped into his suite.

Chapter Two

Big old jerk. Big old hot, handsome, loaded, controlling, scary, uptight, overdressed, kind of sexy if he were a little *nicer* jerk.

This did not bode well for Villa Pietro, Kyra thought, nibbling on her lip and pulling a thread on the antique sofa in the lobby. Things didn't look bright for her beloved Sebastiani family with this nasty new owner.

The whole family had been in an absolute tizzy since they'd gotten the news the new American owner was flying over for a visit. *What does it mean? Why would he come? What will happen to us?*

Anamaria broke out her finest alabaster rosary that Pope John Paul himself had blessed. Lorenzo and Elena locked themselves in the office and dragged out every medal awarded by the Italian Sommelier Association over the last two decades. Enzo and Filippa had their heads together, too, in the kitchen of the big house, preparing feasts they would serve on the expansive courtyard patio for their guest of honor, murmuring about their little boys' futures. Antonio checked the cellars so often, Sofia was worried he'd be underground when she went into labor. And Bruno got plastered and stayed out until sunrise.

Well, that wasn't unusual, but the rest of the normally happy, hardworking, God-fearing, family-loving Sebastiani clan were wired tight and scared to death. They loved growing their noble grapes on rough-hewn pergolas set into vertical terraces. They kept their winemaking secrets and prided themselves on the glorious *rosso* and *bianco* and *rosato*, their picturesque villa and exclusive tastings, their festive harvests followed by peaceful winters.

And Kyra loved them, so she would do whatever was necessary to ensure that family—her family now—could continue the fifty-year-old tradition of the Sebastianis running Villa Pietro.

Whatever was necessary…including suck up to the sourpuss owner. That was fine, though, and came with Kyra's job title, the one she basically invented during the week she first visited—and never left—the winery. Loosely translated, she was the "American Tourist Liaison," but in reality, she was the wandering nomad who stepped into a magical family and became part of it, doing whatever needed to be done to help each and every one of them.

It was her job to go between the Sebastiani family and the hordes of mostly American tourists who'd discovered the precious villa and winery high in the hills above Amalfi's top tourist destination, Positano. So it made sense that Kyra would be the one sent to meet and greet the new owner, to butter him up and take him to the dinner that he apparently *forgot* about.

Or, worse, didn't care if he missed.

Yep, it would take a lot more than butter and at least a vat of last year's harvest to warm up that stone-faced hard-ass. They might have to boil him in olive oil.

The front door opened, and she recognized Silvio

Manzi, a driver who worked for a local car service and frequently brought tourists to the winery.

"Hey, Silvio," she said as he wheeled a suitcase and carry-on. "So you picked up Mr. Brannigan in Sorrento, huh?"

Silvio heaved a sigh. "*Sì*."

"What did you think?" she asked, hoping for something positive.

"Not a talker," he said. "But he mentioned that he was going to Pietro tomorrow." He frowned at her, thinking. "He didn't want to go now. What are you doing here? Just greeting him?"

"What do you mean he didn't *want* to go? He's supposed to be there for dinner tonight."

"Does he know that?"

"I just…" She gasped and put her hand over her mouth. She'd never *told* him she was with the winery, dang it. So he just thought she was some random blonde off the street inviting him to dinner.

And he *accepted*.

Standing, she glanced around the corner, half expecting him to come back any minute and change his mind. "I'm taking him up to dinner at Pietro. That's what we'd planned when his assistant sent his schedule to Lorenzo. Of course, Elena wanted him to stay at the house, but his assistant said he had to be at a hotel." Which was probably where the miscommunication came in. "Did he tell you why he was here?" she asked.

Silvio shrugged. "To visit the winery."

"Visit? That's all?" At Silvio's confused look, she asked, "He didn't tell you he's the new owner?"

The young man drew back, his dark eyes wide. "Really?"

"His father used to own it. He was some gazillionaire

who owned movie studios and half of California, bought Pietro from its previous owner, then disappeared and let the Sebastianis continue to run it for twenty-four years. He never showed up, not once. Now he's dead, and here's the new owner." Even though her English was spoken quickly, Silvio got the gist of what she was saying and looked suitably worried.

"So he didn't say what he wanted to do with the winery?" she pressed, standing up. "Move in? Change anything? Expand it? Cut back? Nothing?"

He shook his head, but she wasn't sure if that meant he didn't know or didn't follow the rapid-fire English questions. "Well, whatever he does," she said on a sigh, "Lorenzo and Elena have a plan."

Silvio laughed. "Food and wine cure all?"

"Pretty much," she agreed. The whole winery had essentially come to a screeching halt when they got the news that James Brannigan was coming. The entire family, all the staff, and half the neighbors had launched into a preparation of meals, tours, and general behind-kissing that would make you think Francis himself was coming down from the Vatican in the popemobile.

"You go." She gave him a nudge. "Get his stuff to him in Suite 6. I'm taking him up to Villa Pietro now."

His eyes popped. "You?"

"Yes, me. Why?"

He looked outside. "But I didn't see the Pietro van."

"That beast? Only Bruno can drive that on these roads. My Vespa seats two."

Silvio looked horrified. "I'll drive him, Kyra."

"No! I want to take the scenic route."

"He won't like that."

"He'll love it," she insisted. "That's all part of the big plan to make him fall completely in love with Positano and Villa Pietro and the family." Not that Mr. Stoneface could fall in love with anything.

"And you think that will make him leave things at the winery exactly as they are?"

"We hope."

Silvio shook his head, doubtful. "Just be careful on the Vespa. You do not want to lose him off the back and watch him tumble all the way down to the mountain."

She gave him a sly smile. "That would be one solution to our problems."

At his dropped jaw, she added a playful jab to his shoulder. "Just kidding! Take his bags now. I have to get him up there before Anamaria has a stroke."

He shook his head as he walked away, her sarcasm and English, as it often was with the Italians, lost on him. And it probably wouldn't be any better received on Big Bad Brannigan, no matter how American he was.

She'd have to work as hard as the rest of the family to impress him, but she would. Kyra would do whatever had to be done to ensure that the winery stayed exactly as it was. It was her home now, the only one where she'd ever felt completely loved and wanted.

So what if she shared a two-bedroom stone house on the outskirts of a vineyard with an eighty-one-year-old widow? Anamaria was the *nonna* Kyra had never had, and Villa Pietro was the home she'd always wanted.

Some big lug nut of a billionaire who happened to have a gorgeous face and dreamy dark eyes was not going to blow into her little bit of heaven and ruin the lives of the people she loved most in the whole world.

He came back down to the lobby then, dressed in light linen trousers and a pale blue button-down shirt with the sleeves rolled up enough to show his forearms.

They were lightly tanned, dusted with dark hair, and muscular enough to draw her attention.

"I think there's been a misunderstanding," she said, clearing her throat when the whole impact of him hit her harder than expected.

For a split second, she thought she detected disappointment flicker in his expression, or maybe that was just a man who didn't like things not to go as he'd planned. "How so?"

"I'm with the winery," she said. "Not..." *A pickup in the hotel lobby.*

He inched back a little. "Villa Pietro?"

"Yes," she said with a laugh. "I'm not sure who you thought I was, but I'm the guest liaison. Specifically, I manage relations with the American tourists."

"Oh...I thought..." He shook his head. "I'm not an American tourist."

She swallowed at his clipped tone. "I know that, Mr. Brannigan. But I'm here in an official capacity to greet you and take you to Pietro to meet everyone and have dinner. Your assistant told Lorenzo you were coming today, so we prepared you a dinner."

"My business manager told me the meeting was tomorrow."

"It's a dinner, not a meeting." Maybe the Wolf of Wall Street didn't know the difference.

He retreated a few steps. "There really is no reason to do that."

No, no. She couldn't lose him. She'd promised the family she'd bring him back, and they'd been working noon and night so his arrival would be perfect. This billionaire trust fund baby wouldn't understand that, of course. Probably wouldn't care that he'd put out some peasants who worked his fields.

She'd need to lure him another way, then. She boldly slid her arm through his and gave a little squeeze. "Would you like me to give you a reason?"

He blinked at her and stared, as if he wasn't sure of the right answer and might be a little taken aback by whatever it was.

"Because I guarantee you have never seen a place like Villa Pietro," she said, purposely lowering her voice so he had to come a little closer. "You will walk the paths of the vineyard under the pergolas that grow the grapes, breathing air so crisp and clear, it could make you weep."

He angled his head in doubt, but she wouldn't let that stop her. She had a memorized speech she gave on the tour, and it never failed.

"You've never seen the pergolas of the Amalfi Coast, vines stacked like God's own stairs on the face of the mountain. You've never tasted wine drenched in the taste of the rock and the sea, the flavor kissed by Bacchus himself."

A slow smile pulled at his lips, drawing her attention to his mouth, which she'd failed to notice was beautifully shaped with soft lips despite the stubble of whiskers from his long day of travel. "Bacchus kissed the flavor?" he asked, a tease in his voice.

"The translation is odd, but let me finish."

"By all means."

Her own smile threatened, but probably because she just realized that his eyes weren't that dark, but flecked with gold the exact color of the *biancolella* grapes that Anamaria sometimes sneaked to her at night. "You've never touched the cool limestone of the cellar walls, or inhaled the musty scent of the oak *barriques* fat with the last harvest, aging to perfection."

"I never have," he agreed, his gaze still locked on hers, "done any of that."

She leaned back. "Then what are you waiting for, James?"

"As if I'd say no after that performance."

"No one ever does." She slipped her hand into his and led him out the door, pumped by her first victory.

Chapter Three

A motor scooter. An undersized two-seater. With bald tires, to boot. James let go of the soft, slender hand that had guided him to the street and stared at what he feared might be his transportation up this mountain. Only his male pride and the fact that riding it meant wrapping his legs around the alluring little vixen who'd coaxed him out here kept him from protesting.

Plus, Kyra handed him a helmet and took one for herself, so surely she cared about safety, right?

"When in Positano," she said with that irresistible smile. Only, James needed to resist, or God only knew what else she'd talk him into.

"I take it there's no Uber."

She just laughed and tugged a pink helmet over her blond hair. His helmet was black, fortunately. Pink might have been his line in the sand. "It's perfectly safe if we avoid the trucks," she promised him. "And so much faster and more beautiful. Hop on."

She slid over the seat, tucking the loose part of her dress under her legs.

He took a deep breath of sea-infused air and got behind her, looking for…no, there was nothing to hold on to except the slender waist of the woman in front of him.

She threw a look over her shoulder. "Ready, James?"

Actually, no. He wasn't ready for any of this. Not the air, the bike, or that precious waist on an impossibly *adorable* woman who should be annoying but...wasn't. He shimmied closer, wrapped his hands around her, and gave a nod into her side-view mirror where he could see the expression of anticipation—and maybe a little glimmer of...gloating—in her eyes.

She grinned in silent reply, revved the engine, and whipped out onto the street, almost knocking him all the way to the left and into the ground.

Holy *shit*.

Without thinking, he tightened his grip, hands and legs, earning a soft chuckle he barely heard over the engine and the wind inside the helmet. He stared straight ahead at her shiny pink dome and the tangle of corn-silk waves that fell out of it and over bare shoulders.

What kind of girl rode around the mountains of Italy in a sundress on a scooter? Why did this winery have an American ambassador to greet him and sweep him off his feet and onto her deathtrap of a bike? Did she work for them really, or was she somehow connected to the family? Married into it?

A surprising thud of disappointment accompanied that thought. Because why the hell would he care if Kyra Summers was married? Sure, she was as cute as Christmas and just about as sparkly, but James Brannigan famously dated ice women, preferably with jet-black hair and exotic looks. At least the last three had met those requirements, and now they were...history.

"Look at the view!" she called out, zipping around the next turn and pointing left.

He automatically reached out and pressed that hand back to the handlebar where it belonged, getting a shake of her shoulders in laughter. "Look," she ordered again.

He turned toward the sea to drink in the vista, slightly blocked by pedestrians, more cars, small trucks, and a thousand parked scooters.

"Isn't it pretty?"

"Yes," he agreed, as he had with the driver who'd asked him the same question. "Pretty dangerous."

Another peal of laughter battled with the revving engine.

She veered around a turn and powered up a ribbon of road, zipping through traffic, narrowly avoiding tourists, and generally making him…hold tighter.

After a few minutes, they were out of the thick of town and making their way up a winding mountain road, higher and higher and *higher*. At each blind corner, he cringed, but every time, she maneuvered the bike like it was an extension of her body.

And James sort of relaxed. At least, he was able to breathe and appreciate the stunning views as they got higher.

"That water is the Bay of Salerno," she said, loud enough for him to hear over the engine. "And look all the way out, past the tip of Sorrento. See Capri?"

He squinted into the setting sun, spotting the world-famous island. "Where the Blue Grotto is?" he asked.

"Oh yeah, that's where the tourists go. Would you like to see it?"

"Not if it's a tourist trap."

"But it is the most beautiful place you've ever seen! I'll take you."

She would? Lord knew how she'd suggest they get there—by skydiving, no doubt.

JAMES

She coaxed more speed out of the bike, taking them so high the umbrellas on the beach below were nothing but tiny orange dots on a sliver of white sand. He turned his attention to the smattering of houses along the street, all cut into the mountain and many made of the same limestone-looking rock.

"Not the kind of place I'd expect to find a winery," he mused, leaning all the way into her so she could hear him. And so he could feel the tautness of her muscles and warmth of her skin.

She shot a quick glance over her shoulder. "Don't you know about our vineyards?" she asked, a mix of accusation and disappointment in her voice.

He understood that. After all, he owned the place and had done little more than hand a file to someone he'd hired with orders to figure out how to sell it. And that order, like every other one he issued to his staff, had been followed.

This was about money; he had to remember that.

"That's why I'm here," he said. *For money.* "To know about the vineyard."

She relaxed a bit at that, dropping her shoulders so that her curves pressed against him. Instinctively, his body reacted to the feel of a soft woman against him. He tried to back away, cursing his hormones for not realizing they were in a life-threatening situation. And the last thing he wanted was for her to feel a boner in her back.

She whipped around the next corner, gunning the engine, coming face-to-face with a truck so big it *had* to be illegal on these roads. She swerved out of the way, brushed some bushes on the right, and yelled, "Duck!"

They both did, and the truck's side-view mirror whizzed right overhead.

Dear *God*.

She just barreled forward. "Good reflexes," she called back.

"Good eye," he countered, the flash of a memory toying at the recesses of his brain. He tried to grab hold of it, but the thought was elusive and gone as quickly as any moment of déjà vu. Plus, he was pretty sure he'd never been on a scooter ducking truck mirrors before.

"Not too far now," Kyra promised as the road finally leveled off and was blessedly empty up here. There were a few homes tucked away here and there, but they'd definitely reached the outskirts of civilization near the top of the mountain. "You okay back there?"

"I'm fine." He turned to look down the mountain and literally sucked in a breath at the view. They were at least a half mile above cobalt-blue water, with the pastels of Positano nothing but a blur against the rock and rolling hills. Powder-puff, white clouds were so close, it felt like he could touch them.

"Most beautiful place on earth, don't you think?" she asked, following his gaze as she slowed the bike.

He couldn't argue the possibility. "It must be one of them."

"No, it is. I can guarantee you." She finally stopped the bike where the road split, taking her helmet off and shaking out her hair, a few silky strands tickling his arm. "I've been everywhere, on every continent and in about fifty countries. This is it. The most incredible place on earth. Or, at least, the most magical."

It was...special. Was that why his father wanted him here? The question jolted him, reminding him of why he was here. Not to ride around on motor scooters with fearless women who turned him on without even trying.

JAMES

"I mean, just inhale." She demonstrated, sucking in a noisy breath.

"I know how to sniff."

"Then do it." She jabbed his arm with her fingertips and repeated her deep inhale, this time with her eyes closed. That gave him a chance to really look at her, taking in the delicate lines of her jaw and lips, the slopes of well-defined cheekbones, the feminine arch of her brows.

"Isn't it stunning?" she asked.

She was. Surprisingly so, since he generally avoided blondes, especially bubbly, spirited, talkative, *fun* blondes. So not his type. But she…she intrigued him.

Intrigue. Is that what you're calling it, James? No, it was more arousal than intrigue, if he was going to be honest. And that was not in the cards.

He climbed off the scooter and took his helmet off, wanting to drink in the view again but finding it hard to look away from her. "You've really been in fifty countries?" he asked. "That's impressive."

"Fifty at least, but some for only a few hours. Still, the Amalfi Coast is the best. It's home for me now." There was nothing but pride in her voice.

"Where are you from?" he asked, fully expecting the answer to be Southern California. She had *Malibu Beach girl* stamped all over her, the kind his surfer brother, Knox, would have hit on so hard the poor girl wouldn't be able to stop laughing as she ripped off her clothes. Knox wasn't stripping beach girls anymore, though. Yoga girls, and only one.

"I never know how to answer that question," Kyra said. "I was born in Ohio, lived in five, six…maybe seven states. I lost track. I've been traveling since I turned eighteen, so twelve years. But I'm here now." She waved her hand with the gesture of someone showing off her very own living room. "Home."

She said the word with reverence, a soft whisper heavy with meaning, so much tenderness in her voice that he didn't know how to respond.

"It's…nice."

She choked softly. "This is what I was most afraid of. What we all were afraid of."

He frowned at her. "Afraid of?"

"You don't get it."

"How pretty it is here?" He shrugged and glanced around. "I get it."

"No, you don't *get* it. And you *own* it." She closed her eyes and shook her head, guiding the bike to a wall and leaning it there, taking the keys. "Come on, James Brannigan. We have work to do."

"Work?"

She smiled up at him. "Not you. Us. The Sebastiani family. The caretakers of your winery."

It wouldn't be his for long. He walked next to her, down a stone path lined with thick bushes and more of those pink and purple flowers. "These are everywhere," he mused, touching one.

"Bougainvillea," she said. "The official flower of Positano. Come on." She nudged him around a corner. "We're almost there."

He blinked into the fading light, making out the lines of a huge gray stone structure jutting out from the mountain. It was three stories in the front, but only one in the back, with a dozen arched windows and two turrets. In front of it were massive terraces of vineyards, the grapes growing on rows of sticks that seemed to go on for an acre. Five, no, six layers down the side of the mountain like massive green stairs.

Smaller stone buildings dotted the view, similar in style and structure, all somehow both humble and impressive. The earth was a blend of green and brown, and the air was heavy with the scents of lemons and olives and herbs. All of it, perched on the edge of the world, as high as the clouds.

"Don't tell me," she said, a hint of sarcasm in her voice. "It's...*pretty*."

"Pretty...overwhelming." He spoke softly, because he suddenly felt like he'd stepped on something sacred. Which was ridiculous, but that's how he felt.

"Now we're getting there," she murmured.

He didn't know if she meant the response or the destination, but he followed as they walked a hundred yards or so to an iron gate that led to another path with a wood and gold sign that said *Villa Pietro*.

He stood stone-still, and so did Kyra, possibly for the first time since he met her. He felt her gaze on him as intently as his was on the remarkable view in front of him.

"What do you think?" she asked on a whisper.

"I think—"

"Brannigan!" The word echoed like a bullet shot over the mountain, followed by a loud scream from one, no, two, tiny boys who quite literally dropped out of a tree and started running toward him. "*Braaaannnnnigan!*" they repeated.

What the—

They were on him in a second, one leaping into his arms and the taller one wrapping himself around James's legs and hanging on for dear life.

"Nico! Gianni! *Smettetela*! Stop!" Kyra's command was lost in the screaming and hugging and full-body assault that almost knocked him on his ass. She rattled off more Italian, taking the arm of the taller boy and helping to free James. "He is not a new playmate," she said, trying to sound stern but laughing.

James chuckled, too, surprising himself with the sudden burst of familiarity that came with the loud onslaught of little boys.

Finally, the one in James's arms scrambled down, his little face looking up with a smile of pure expectation. "*Signor* Brannigan," he said, barely able to catch his breath. "*Benvenuto a Villa Pietro!*"

The little one let go, arching back to peer up at James with the biggest, darkest, most soulful eyes he'd ever seen. "Welcome," he said in tentative, practiced English. "We have waited for you."

They had? He tore his gaze from the precious little face to meet Kyra's smile, her own enthusiastic greeting of how long they'd waited coming back to him. He'd thought she meant the hotel, but she meant…this. Them. The *winery*. The family.

They'd been waiting for the owner to show, and suddenly, deep in his gut, he knew that the last thing they would want to hear was that he was selling the place out from under them.

Chapter Four

Kyra peeled the boys off their victim, laughing and chastising them in a mix of Italian and the English they seemed to pick up so easily since she'd moved here.

"Nico! Let him breathe."

The child squirmed away, still holding James's hand. "*Vieni, vieni Signor Brannigan! Vieni!*"

"He wants you to come with him." She took Gianni's hand as he pulled her forward.

"*La famiglia sta aspettando!*" Gianni exclaimed.

"He says his family is waiting. This is Gianni Sebastiani." She held up his hand. "And you have Nico Sebastiani. They are the sons of Enzo and Filippa, and the official welcoming committee to Villa Pietro."

A slow smile lifted James's lips, surprising her. "Let me guess. You're...seven?" He pointed to Gianni.

"*Sette*," she translated. "Seven years old, *sì*?"

"*Sì*. I be seven," he said slowly, beaming with pride over his English.

"And." James took a good long look at Nico. "Five?" he guessed.

Nico's eyes widened, and he slowly shook his head.

"Tell him your age," Kyra said. "*Quanti anni hai.*"

"*Quattro*," he whispered, his shyness kicking in now that he had to speak on his own.

"Ahh. Four." James nodded—and still held Nico's hand, Kyra noticed. "You look a little older."

She eyed him, curious, and suddenly, something dawned on her. "You have children, James?"

"No, no," he said quickly. "But I have a small battalion of younger brothers, six of them, to be exact. So I'm not a novice with little boys."

For some reason, that made her heart lighter. Seven boys? Surely he understood the power of family, and if he got that, then maybe he wouldn't do anything to hurt or change this one.

Gianni pulled on Kyra's hand, tugging her closer to whisper in her ear. "Is he nice?" he asked in Italian.

Remains to be seen, she thought. But she didn't answer, instead leaning over to speak to both of them. "Boys, you remember your promise."

They nodded. "English only for *Signor* Brannigan," they replied in unison.

"Impressive," James said. "How did you learn English so young?"

They didn't answer right away, their little faces registering the attempt to translate every word.

"I taught them," Kyra told him. "And they're excellent students. Come now." She urged them toward the path that led to the house. "The entire Sebastiani family is waiting. Lead the way, boys!"

Gianni and Nico broke away, running ahead.

"Cute kids," James said. "Are there more?"

"No more little ones, but plenty of Sebastianis. But don't worry, I've taught them all quite a bit of English, and they all want to impress you. A lot. Maybe too much. You might want to brace yourself," she added.

He slowed his step, his attention on her more than the winery, a look of interest and maybe a little admiration in his eyes. "You've taught them all English?"

"I've been trying since I got here. They want so much to learn."

"How long have you been with the winery?" he asked.

"I came for a tour eighteen months ago," she said, smiling at the memory. "And I never left."

He lifted both brows. "Must have been some tour."

"It was love at first sight."

"Then it must have been some tour *guide*."

That made her laugh. "No, it was love with the vineyard and winery, not anyone in particular. And, to be honest, the tour was terrible. The Sebastiani family are master vintners, with two renowned enologists in the family, but they didn't know squat about dealing with visitors. As a professional tourist, I made some suggestions that Elena and Lorenzo really liked."

"Elena and Lorenzo?" he asked.

She stifled a sigh of frustration. "You really didn't do your homework, did you?"

"I have people who do my homework."

La-di-da. "Okay, here's the rundown. Pay attention, it's all going to come at you very fast."

"Okay. I'm a quick study."

He seemed more relaxed now. Much better on two feet and solid ground than he'd been clinging to her on the bike. Not that she'd minded his strong hands on her waist or the pressure of his body against her back. Nope, didn't mind that at all.

"Okay, the older woman you will meet is Anamaria, who was married to Giorgio Sebastiani, who was the caretaker and vintner since 1966, but he died two years ago. Don't mention his name, or she'll cry. And don't ask her how old she is, or she'll—"

"Shove a garlic clove down my throat."

She put a hand on his arm, delighted. "Oh, you *have* done your homework."

"My driver mentioned it," he said.

"Well, he's absolutely correct. But don't be scared of her. She's quite sweet and has been saying rosaries for you since we found out you were coming."

"Really. Then I guess my altar-boy experience will impress the hell out of her."

She angled her head at the choice of words. "So to speak. And you can call her Anamaria or Nonna, and her English might surprise you. I've been teaching her since we live together."

He turned to her. "You live here, too?"

"Anamaria and I share the northernmost house." As they reached a small rise in the path, she pointed. "See those three stone structures on the other side of the main house? Anamaria and I live in the smallest one. The big one in the middle is Filippa, Enzo, and the boys'. Enzo is Lorenzo and Elena's oldest son."

"You mentioned them, but…" He gave her a questioning look.

"Lorenzo is Anamaria and Giorgio's son, and Elena is his wife, and they are the official caretakers of the winery now. Are you confused yet?"

"Borderline."

"Then hang on, because there are more Sebastianis. Antonio, Lorenzo's younger brother, is married to Sofia, and they live in the last house."

He studied the landscape intently, as if memorizing the visual and the names. "Sofia's pregnant with a girl."

She stopped and beamed at him, an unexpected warmth filling her. "My, you are a fast study."

"Keep teaching me," he said. "We're almost there. Who lives in the big house?"

"Lorenzo and Elena have the upstairs apartment, with Bruno, their youngest son."

"Ah, Bruno. Every family has one."

She hooted softly. "Only if they're unlucky. What else did Silvio tell you?"

"Not much," he said, sliding a look at her. "He certainly didn't mention you."

Something in the way he made the comment, a little sly, a little bit flirtatious even, made Kyra's heart stutter. "Lorenzo is a master enologist and the brains behind the operation. Enzo runs the business end and also happens to be a great cook, and Antonio has a degree in enology and has been certified in viticulture."

"So they aren't just...country farmers." He seemed surprised by that.

"They are bright, hardworking, wonderful people who have been the caretakers of Villa Pietro since the 1960s. Wine is their life and family..." She smiled, thinking of the phrase she'd heard a thousand times since she'd arrived. *La famiglia è tutto.* "Family is everything."

They turned the last corner before the long set of stone stairs up to the house. The boys were waiting at the top, blocking the entrance to the courtyard. She knew that the entire family would be waiting in the large open patio where they had parties, held tastings, and gathered tour groups.

He paused at the bottom and looked up, taking in the grandeur of the main house, where so much of the winery's business took place. His gaze drifted over the mountainside, lingering on the rows and rows of vine-covered pergolas plunging halfway down to the sea.

What must it be like to look at this slice of paradise and know that you *own* it? An ache she didn't even understand squeezed her chest. Fear for the family, of course. Fear of change. Her lifelong fear of yet another upheaval.

Without thinking, she put her hand on his arm again, adding some pressure, not surprised that his bicep was well developed and hard. "James," she said softly.

He turned to her.

"Don't hurt them."

A flicker of something she didn't know how to interpret flashed in his eyes. Surprise or disappointment that she would make that request? Or was it a warning she saw? As if he knew he was about to do just that.

Even with Kyra's lesson, the names and faces ran together in James's head, one big blur of dark eyes, big smiles, loud laughs, flying hands, and an onslaught of Italian greetings. Before James had a chance to look around the expansive patio and drink in the jaw-dropping scenery, he had a thick stemless glass of wine shoved into his hand and a mix of questions and comments and broken English coming at him.

Kyra stayed close, translated with ease, and even kept the wild little boys at bay when they got close and stared up at him like he'd dropped down from Mars. But after the initial excitement died off and they'd all had their chance to show off some English phrases, James started to size up the family. There was the de facto leader, fiftysomething Lorenzo with his salt-and-pepper hair and keen brown eyes, and his soft-spoken but sharp-eyed wife, Elena. Two more serious-seeming sons, with lovely wives—one looking like she'd pop any second—the little guys, and the quiet, brooding Bruno.

But it was the tiny white-haired woman they called *Nonna* who interested James the most. Anamaria Sebastiani couldn't have been four feet ten inches. She literally stood at the height of James's chest, and he had to bend over to speak to her.

When he did, she looked up—way up—and he sensed the entire family holding its collective breath as she studied him with an unwavering golden-brown gaze. Her skin was surprisingly smooth, he noticed, her hair still thick and wavy. She wore a clean white apron over her clothes, and something told him she never took it off.

"Hello, *Signora* Sebastiani," he said again when she didn't speak and her scrutiny became a little uncomfortable for everyone. "It's a pleasure to meet you."

"The father. *Padre*. Father."

He blinked, completely unsure of what she meant by that. Remembering Kyra's comment about the rosary, he wondered if the sight of him had her praying. Maybe he should play the altar-boy card now.

Kyra stepped closer and said something in Italian, but the old woman held up a hand as if to quiet her. And everyone. And still, she stared.

"You"—she turned a crooked, veiny finger on him—"look like the father."

"The...father?"

"Colin. Colin Brannigan."

Even with her thick accent, he understood that. And felt the whole family share looks of worry and concern. All they got from Anamaria was a wave as if she sensed that same worry and it didn't bother her a bit.

"*Che occhi.*" Using two fingers, she pointed to her eyes, and again, he was confused. Did she mean she could see the resemblance or that James shared his father's eye color?

"Do you remember him well?" he asked.

"*Sì, sì.* I remember him. And her," she said, obviously understanding more English than she spoke. "He was a…a…" She dug for a word, then turned to Kyra and rattled off a long string of Italian. Kyra's eyes widened ever so slightly, and she nodded.

"Say!" Anamaria ordered, pointing that busy, gnarled hand to James. "Tell!"

Kyra turned and gave a slightly apologetic smile. "She said your father was very handsome. And you are, too."

"Oh." He grinned, mostly at the color rising in Kyra's pretty cheeks. "Thanks."

Anamaria added something, insistent, poking Kyra's shoulder and making everyone else laugh.

"Something tells me you're not giving a full translation," James said to Kyra.

"She says she's sorry for your loss. We all are."

James might not understand Italian, but he knew she was not telling the whole truth, because they wouldn't laugh at that. "Thank you," he said, then narrowed his eyes. "Now tell me what she really said."

"That you are very sexy."

He laughed and leaned closer to the old woman, who looked at him with an expression somewhere between salacious and smug. "You're too kind," he said.

"And your smile is from the mother." The old woman pressed her hands together and lit from the inside. "Kathy."

For a moment, James was speechless. Maybe it was

because he didn't remember his mother being called anything but Kathleen. Or maybe because he'd been expecting this family to know only his father, who had been, in essence, their boss. But of course, Mom and Dad had come here together once, before Dad had purchased the winery, about six or eight months before Mom died. So, if this old woman remembered Dad, she remembered his mother, too.

With the exception of his Aunt Claire, few people in James's life talked about his mother. Coming face-to-face with someone who'd met her and remembered her took him aback, for some reason.

"Kathleen," he corrected automatically. She'd hated the nickname Kathy.

But Anamaria shook her head. "Kathy," she insisted. "That is what I call her. She was lovely woman and...and..." She turned to Kyra and gestured. "Like my *Cara*. How do you say?" She ran her finger in front of her face, as if drawing a smile. "Happy. Always, always happy."

Yes, she was. Mom had exuded joy like no one he'd ever met. He glanced to the woman next to him, whose blue eyes took in every nuance of the exchange. No one he'd ever met *until now*. "I remember her that way, too," he said.

"But no girl," Anamaria added, sounding a little disgusted. "Just boy babies. Seven."

He nodded. "No girls, but I'm sure they hoped every time."

Anamaria stepped closer, lifting up on her tiptoes. "She tried here. Every night, they try."

"Mamma!"

"Nonna!"

Unaffected by the chastising from her family, the

little woman raised her narrow shoulders, turned down her mouth, and nodded. "Happy, though. So she must like trying for the baby girl. Always the laughing. Like my Kyra," she repeated.

"I can see that. She was like you," he said to Kyra. "Very...enthusiastic."

Was that why bubbly blondes never did it for him? He didn't get a chance to wallow in that self-analysis or the news that Mom and Dad had ever considered an eighth child, because Lorenzo stepped forward and Elena gently eased Anamaria away.

Kyra and Lorenzo flanked James, and with the rest of the family falling behind in a way that almost seemed choreographed or practiced, they walked him across the courtyard, announcing that it was time for the tour.

Yes, they'd definitely worked hard to impress him. And once again, James was pinged with some guilt over what he'd really come to Italy to do.

Chapter Five

He was an exemplary guest, Kyra thought as they reached the cellars after a long, slow tour through the rustic main house. Except for the fact that he never took one sip of the Pietro Rosso Riserva, one of their best wines, he asked questions and showed interest in every aspect of the winery's business. Like so many guests and tourists, he was fascinated by the "vertical" winery and the many varieties of grapes that grew on the acres of decades-old trellises along the mountainside.

Amalfi wine was like no other, and Kyra spoke with pride as she explained how the vines grew into the soil under the rock—where the name "Pietro" came from—and how that rock gave the grapes a unique and earthy flavor.

He spent a long time in the cellars, listening intently as Antonio explained the winemaking process and detailed, with Kyra's help, the blend of old-school technique and modern technology that they'd brought into the business.

The group broke up after that, off to prepare the tasting room, while Kyra and James took another walk through the highest level of the vineyard so he could have a chance to taste the *casavecchia* grapes that Antonio had talked so much about.

"You seem surprised at the level of up-to-date equipment we use," she commented as they ducked under some low-hanging branches.

"I really don't know a lot about the process of making wine," he said. "And this place looks so authentic and old, it's surprising to see a state-of-the-art destemmer and crush pad in action when I half expect to see the family stomping on the grapes in their bare feet."

"We do some of that for the tourists at harvest time," she assured him. "But don't you know what machinery is purchased? Lorenzo doesn't make any major financial moves without consulting the owner."

"The owner's *business manager*," he corrected. "And remember, I've only had this winery in my portfolio for eight months. I assume my father knew about the improvements and technology, but I honestly haven't had time to look into it."

"And that's why you're here?" she asked.

He turned to her, his expression solemn as he didn't answer right away. "Partially," he said.

"To learn about our business." She made it a statement, because that's what she wanted to be true. "Right?" she added when he didn't answer.

"I'm here to...see everything," he said.

She let out a breath, relieved. Not here to *sell* everything. "Well, I'm glad you're here," she said brightly. "I think the owner of the business should show up periodically, and it's always bothered Anamaria that your father never came back after all those years."

He nodded. "It sounded like he and my mother had quite the, uh, romantic getaway here."

"Anamaria is nothing if not blunt and honest, in any language."

"Wait until I tell Finn he might not have been last in our long line of boys."

"Finn is number seven, I take it?" she asked, relieved to have the conversation momentarily off the fate of the winery. "What are their names, these six brothers of yours?"

"In order? I'm the oldest. And then there's Gabe, who, I guess, I'm closest to."

"You guess?"

"We're not a particularly close family."

"What a shame," she said. "I would think seven brothers would be so much fun."

He considered that for a second. More than a second. "We were, once," he said almost under his breath. "But now…" He shrugged. "Anyway, Gabe is the most like me."

"How so?" she asked.

"He has his head on straight and knows a good business deal when he sees it. He has a twin, Hunter, who's pretty much the opposite and lives to be a pain in the rear. Succeeds at that, most of the time, too."

She smiled, thinking of Bruno. "Who else?"

"After Gabe and Hunter, there's Max, a Navy SEAL badass. Then Luke, who never met an adventure he couldn't turn into a documentary. Knox, our resident party boy, is second to the end, and last is Finn." He grinned. "The baby who flies fighter jets, or did. So I guess I should stop thinking of him as a baby."

All those Brannigans. And all so impressive. What would it be like to be raised in a home like that? That was something Kyra, who moved from one sterile, lonely, isolated high-end apartment to the next with nothing but the revolving door of nannies to keep her company, would never know.

"It sounds wonderful, that big family. I'm jealous."

He gave a soft snort. "Don't be. It wasn't easy to corral that crew growing up, and the hard stuff fell to me."

"Because you're the oldest?" she asked.

"And because my mother died when I was twelve, less than a year after she and my dad came here."

Kyra tried to imagine the impact of that loss on a twelve-year-old boy with six siblings and failed.

"I'm sorry for your whole family." And then she bit her lip, a thought occurring to her. "Do you think that's why your father never came back to Positano?"

He reached out to touch a grape hanging in a thick bunch from the pergola above them. "I don't know the history. I don't know why he bought it or…" He looked directly at her. "Why he gave it to me."

"Probably because he loved you."

He gave a wry smile. "My dad always had a strange way of showing that."

She gestured behind her, toward the house. "What did he say about it when he was alive? Did he reminisce about being here with your mom? Did they have pictures in an album? Did he ever hint he might leave it to you someday?"

"No one knew he owned it until he died." He plucked a grape. "Can I eat this?"

Her jaw dropped. No one knew? Why not? Who would hide this place? "Well…that explains why he never came here," she said on a sigh, reaching up for the grape. "*Falanghina*." She took one for herself. "It's one of my favorites."

He popped the fruit in his mouth, and she did, too, his eyes widening at the sweetness.

"But you're here now," she said after swallowing.

JAMES

"And that's all that matters. A Brannigan owner has arrived and now..."

He studied her for a moment, silent and expectant, as if he waited to see what she thought he would do. But he certainly didn't finish the sentence for her.

"And now it's time to taste the *bianco* wine this grape makes," she finished.

"I don't drink wine."

Oh Lord. Another jaw-dropper of an announcement.

"Ironic, isn't it?" he said, smiling at her reaction.

"Insane, more like. You have to taste the wine." Her voice rose in a little bit of panic. "You can't appreciate Villa Pietro if you don't taste the wine."

"I don't drink," he said simply.

She blinked at him, wondering why, but knowing it would be rude to ask.

"I don't do anything that makes me lose control."

"So you don't...do roller coasters or fast cars or downhill skiing?"

"None of the above."

Really? "Nothing that makes you just want to close your eyes, hang on, and let go of control?"

"Never."

That couldn't be true. "You don't have sex?" she challenged.

He choked a soft laugh. "I didn't say that."

"That's exactly what you said."

He eyed her, the smile lingering on his face and adding a twinkle to his eye. "I stay in control. Always. Even with a woman. Especially with a woman." He inched ever so slightly closer, holding her gaze, making her stomach flip like *she* was the one on a roller coaster, in a fast car, or flying down a ski slope. "She's the one who loses control."

For a moment, she couldn't breathe. Couldn't think, actually. Couldn't do anything but imagine what that would be like. "Too bad for you," she said with remarkable lightness.

"Why?"

"It's fun to lose control."

"Fun isn't a priority for me," he said, plucking another grape, turning from her to take in the view or maybe shift the subject. "And I'm really not sure what my father was thinking when he made the decision to give me this winery knowing that about me, and the fact that I'm not the least bit interested in wine."

"Did he say anything about the inheritances he'd planned before he died?" she asked.

"I had no idea my father was sick, let alone holed up in the Bahamas selectively choosing seven different parting gifts to confuse and confound his sons."

She frowned, watching a storm brew in his eyes, gone as quickly as it had arrived. "So, you all got something like this winery?" she asked.

"Something. The entire estate won't be divided up for years, but when he died, my father gave each of us a 'legacy,' and we have to…deal with it."

"What do you mean, deal with it?"

He lifted a shoulder as if to say it would be too hard to explain. "It depended on whether it was property, a business, or an item. Like, Knox got a vintage motorcycle, and Hunter ended up with a treasure map."

"Did he find the treasure?"

"He found a ring and put it on the right finger of a woman who helped him find it. Or should I say left, third one?"

She smiled at that, but she was more concerned about

his legacy than the others. "So, how are you going to 'deal with' Villa Pietro?"

He opened his mouth to speak, then closed it, his precious control obviously taking charge of whatever he planned to say. Instead, he reached out and touched the cluster of grapes again, quiet.

"James?" she prodded.

"I'm dealing with it right now," he finally said. "Touring the place and…"

"*Tasting* the wine."

He angled his head and gave her a wry smile. "You want me to break my personal code for the sake of a sip of white wine."

"Not any white wine. This is Pietro Fiorduva, which has won the coveted Tre Bicchieri award five years in a row," she said. "You may never taste anything quite like it again."

He stared at her for a long time, not answering, studying her face intently, and she could feel her argument losing ground in the face of his determination. He *had* to taste the wine, she thought. He wouldn't experience Pietro if he didn't taste the wine.

Before he could answer, she leaned a little closer.

"James," she whispered.

"Why do I feel another tour guide speech coming on?"

Because it was. Undaunted, she looked right into his eyes. "I promise nothing so perfect will touch your lips while you are in Italy."

A shadow of a smile curved those very lips, and he surprised her by moving his hand from the grapes to her face. He brushed her lower lip with his thumb, sending a thousand chill bumps up her arms and down her spine.

"Don't be so sure of that, Kyra."

For a long moment, the only thing she was aware of was…him. Not the crystal-clean air laden with the earthy scent of the vineyard or the brush of a breeze over the grape leaves. Just sexy James Brannigan who was…flirting with her. Pretty damn hard.

He finally tipped his head toward the house. "I guess one taste won't hurt."

"No," she agreed on a sigh. "It won't hurt at all."

In fact, it might feel really, really good.

Chapter Six

James rolled over on the plush king-sized bed, suddenly, viciously wide awake. Must have been the damn wine. There was a reason he didn't touch the stuff, and this was it.

But he hadn't had enough of the liquid-gold silk they called Fiorduva or the deep, ruby *rosso*—even though he had agreed to taste every one of the award-winning vintages they'd put in front of him—to feel the effects.

No, this wasn't a drinker's three a.m. wake-up call, though that was the precise time on the screen of his cell phone. Nor was this jet lag, something he rarely suffered, anyway.

James pushed up and frowned into the darkness.

This was…loss of control. He knew this out-of-sorts ache of frustration that plagued him down to the bones. He didn't feel in control of this whole situation.

For instance, what kept him from looking Lorenzo Sebastiani in the eye last night and telling him exactly what he'd planned to tell him: *I'm selling this winery.* Something had stopped him.

Was it uncertainty? Doubt? Or was it a blond sprite who made him laugh and drink wine and ride a scooter through sun-washed hills and think about…sex?

That was another aspect that felt a little out of his control. The low-grade hum of want that buzzed through him when he was near Kyra. And now, when he wasn't.

He threw back the covers and climbed out of bed, snapping the waistband of the boxers he'd slept in, but not bothering to find anything else to wear. He walked into the wide hallway of the suite, following it into the expanse of the luxurious living room lit only by moonlight pouring in through a set of double French doors that led to the balcony.

Pushing them open, he stepped outside to a full moon high over the Mediterranean Sea and the glittering lights from the homes and buildings on the mountainside. A few yachts bobbed along the black horizon, the dark water glinting like it had been dusted with diamonds.

But he barely saw the view. In fact, he closed his eyes and the only thing he saw were bright blue eyes rimmed in dark lashes, pearly white teeth, and dimples so deep and cute he just wanted to…taste them.

Oh holy hell, he was going to make a decision this big with his dick? So he met a hot woman who made him act a little out of character. Hell, it was Italy. People went crazy here, with the food and wine and moon and flowers. Look what happened to Dad. One trip and the son of a bitch bought a winery.

But it wasn't just her. It was *them*. The whole lot of noisy, drinky, happy Italians who'd built a world around Villa Pietro. They reminded him of…Brannigans.

Old Brannigans. Before Mom died.

Not that the families were anything alike, but there was an unspoken unity, something he could interpret in any language. They were a strong family, he could tell. What would the sale of the winery do to them?

Nothing, he reminded himself. They'd all be well

compensated. He'd make sure Whitehouse took care of the people who'd taken care of the winery. Lorenzo would have a retirement fund, and Antonio would have money for the baby girl when she was…

"Good Lord," he muttered, leaning against the balcony. What the hell was *wrong* with him? It was this place. It made him crazy. It made him worry about people he'd known for less than twelve hours.

What he needed was someone to make him sane. Someone to talk some sense into him and remind him that he could do whatever the hell he wanted with the legacy his father left.

"Gabe," he murmured, turning to go back to the bedroom to get his phone. "Gabe gets it." And it was six in the evening in California, so his brother should be available.

He picked up his phone, surprised to see a text had come in while he'd been on the balcony. He tapped the screen and cursed the little jolt of surprise at the first words. Surprise and pleasure. Of course, he'd given Kyra a number to contact him but hadn't expected that contact to be made at three in the morning.

We're hosting a special tour tomorrow for a small group from the States. Would you join us? It will be different from today and we thought it would be good for you to see how well our tourist business runs. She added a little happy-face emoji and a cluster of grapes. And a thumbs-up. And a glass of red wine, the Italian flag, the American flag, a scooter, a sun with a face, and a little pink heart.

And what did he do?

He smiled.

At *emojis*. He couldn't think of a single person he texted who used those things, or imagine why the sight of them would amuse him. But that's what Kyra did. She amused him. And, he thought, aroused him.

He couldn't let that cloud his thinking. Without responding to her text, he called the brother he was closest to, both in age and temperament. Hunter, Gabe's twin, might be the same age, but sharing a birthday was all those two had in common.

Gabe picked up on the first ring. "James, you son of a bitch. Where are you?"

The greeting didn't surprise him, but there was something different in Gabe's voice that he'd noticed for the last few months. Must be his new wife who made him sound less focused and driven.

"Positano, Italy."

"Sounds glamorous. And, what the hell? Has to be the middle of the night there."

James headed back to the balcony, drawn to the fresh air and mystical view. "Dead middle. Three a.m. and I can't sleep."

"Since when does Perfect James sleep?" he joked, using the brothers' favorite nickname for him. "Hong Kong markets open up in half an hour. You should be getting your next deal lined up, slacker. Is something up?"

"Why didn't you sell the ranch?" James asked, the question coming out with unexpected speed and urgency. He hadn't realized just how much he wanted an answer to that until now.

Gabe didn't hesitate. "I told you when you were out here for our wedding. Josephine and I are fixing it up. It's a cool project, making it new. And get this. I spent the weekend redoing that tree house. Do you remember the one Dad built, and Mom spent hours making those damn curtains? Remember how we teased her? Like seven boys cared about curtains."

JAMES

James closed his eyes, blocking out the moon-washed water for another beautiful image in his head. Mom, talking around pins clamped between her lips, hanging blue and white curtains over the windows that really existed for the sole purpose of bracing a toy gun aimed at another brother. But Mom insisted that the tree house have curtains.

"Why would you fix that thing up?" James asked. "I mean, unless you've come to your senses and are selling that property, which is worth a small fortune."

His brother laughed softly. "Don't need or want a small fortune, and this ranch has too many good memories."

Memories? Of noisy boys and missing fathers and disappearing mothers? "Since when did memories matter to you, Gabe?"

"They matter. And Josephine and I plan to make even more."

"Really." James tried to visualize his brother in his usual habitat—in a suit, game face on, behind a desk, juggling at least four high-end real estate deals, keeping an eye on his ever-growing bank account.

When Gabe didn't respond, James wondered if they'd lost the call. "You there?"

"Yeah, sorry, I was just walking out to the koi pond to give something to Josephine."

The *koi pond*? "Quitting work early today?" James asked.

"Oh hell, I blew today off. We rode horses half the day."

What? "Why?"

"Uh, because I felt like it, and it was fun. Hey, I'm going to see Knox and Erin tonight before they leave for Yosemite. Did you know they're going up to visit Luke and Lizzie? You should call us later, and we can all talk."

What the hell? Since when did they do family group chats? Family anything other than Gabe's wedding last year, and a lackluster email chain that he barely looked at.

"No calls, I'm too busy," James said. "But, listen, I still want to know what was it about the deal on the ranch and the real reason you didn't sell. I never knew you to pass up a payoff like that, Gabe."

"I told you the real reason...." His voice drifted off. Was he at the koi pond again? James's frustration grew, which was weird with Gabe. He was the only one of all six brothers who thought and acted just like James. And now? James didn't know who Gabe was anymore. Riding horses in the middle of a workday. Had marriage changed him that much?

Something had.

"Never mind," James said, pushing up from the chair he'd taken.

"No, I want to tell you," Gabe said. "I already have more money than I know what to do with. God knows, you do, too, but, stick with me now, okay?"

Maybe. Maybe not. "Okay."

"Coming here showed me a side of Dad I'd forgotten existed. Do you remember him happy?"

James didn't answer, closing his eyes for a second to try to picture Colin Brannigan happy.

"He was once," Gabe continued. "He was happy when Mom was here with us."

Yes, he was. Everyone was. The whole damn family.

"A piece of him died when she did, James. I didn't see that until I came back here. I understand now that there was more to him. And, there are some things you can't put a price on, you know? I think…"

"Yeah?" James asked when Gabe dragged that thought out too long.

"I think Dad wanted me to know that."

James looked skyward. Gabe wasn't helping at all. "Speaking of prices, I'm here in Italy saddled with this winery and I know he wanted me to get the best possible price for it. So, I wondered if there were some legalities or fine-print issues that stopped you from doing the same thing with the ranch."

Gabe laughed again, not his old, wry laugh, either. This was warmer. "No fine print, bro. I found someone I want to spend the rest of my life with, and this ranch will always be part of our story. My children will ride ATVs up and down the trails just like we did."

His children? What the hell?

"Give the winery a chance," Gabe said, oblivious to James's shock. "Something you want might be there."

"There's nothing I want here." Except one hella hot woman. "I'll figure it out," he finally said. "I already have an offer for the place."

"Then what's stopping you?"

"Nothing," he answered quickly. "Nothing's stopping me."

"So, keep me posted," Gabe said. "And I'll tell Knox you said hi."

"Except I didn't. How is that little rebel?"

"Hasn't been little for a long time, big brother, and he's not much of a rebel anymore. Call him sometime. It's important that we all talk."

James looked at the phone, wondering if he'd somehow called the wrong man. "Sure thing, Gabe. Thanks."

"You bet. Stay in touch."

When he hung up, he stared at that emoji-filled text

again, still rooting around for a sense of control that he couldn't find.

Thanks for nothing, Gabe.

He strode back to the bedroom, turned on the light, and stood at the long desk that he'd already loaded with papers and his laptop, lifting the Whitehouse Wineries documentation. Flipping the file open, he narrowed his eyes at the price they'd offered.

"Shit," he murmured. "That place?" It was worth fifty percent more than the dollar amount on the page. All that land. Those incredible cellars. The equipment and pergolas and stair-step vineyards and…family.

He swallowed and shook his head. Who the hell agreed to a price that low? They were giving that property away, and that was not how James rolled at the negotiation table.

He flipped through the supporting documentation that he hadn't even really studied. Things were missing, or bare-bones. This wouldn't do at all. He didn't know Dad's sideways logic for giving him this winery, and maybe he never would. But he was James Brannigan, and that meant he took control and made a huge profit. And with this deal, he would demand both, even if it prolonged the process a little.

Picking up his phone, he ignored Kyra's text and sent another one to William Hayward, the business manager he'd hired to handle the winery and its sale.

Go back to the negotiation table with Whitehouse. I'm raising the price. Get me the description of liens, a discretionary earnings and cash flow statement, supplier and distribution contracts, financial ratios and trends, an asset depreciation schedule by tomorrow. I'll review those and set a new price.

Then he went back to bed, knowing he'd sleep now.

Chapter Seven

Kyra woke a few hours after sunrise and donned one of her favorite dresses for the busy day with tourists that lay ahead. Tourists and…James?

She checked her phone again as she finished scrunching her curls and applying a bit of makeup, thinking about the invitation she'd sent in the middle of the night. And the fact that he'd ignored it.

Now what? He'd left yesterday with a vague promise that he'd be back, or Lorenzo would hear from someone in his company. Did that mean James was leaving? After one dinner? Yes, it had been warm and delightful, and he'd seemed to relax, especially after the tasting.

She liked him relaxed, she thought as she slipped on some sandals. The man was hot no matter what his mood, she couldn't deny that. She got lost a few times in those smoky dark eyes that seemed to linger on her for one heartbeat too long. His hair was thick and dark, but had the occasional golden streak that made her want to reach out and grab a handful. He was muscular and strong, but even at six feet or so, he moved with the grace of a man who had complete control over his body.

He did, she reminded herself. Control over everything. Including this winery.

James Brannigan was very sexy in that New York businessman with oodles of money and too much power kind of way.

A type that didn't interest her in the least.

But when he laughed? When he forgot about money, power, and control, and actually tried to play bocce and let Nico win? Her heart melted. A few other parts got warm, too, she had to admit.

She left her stone cottage and headed to the main house, knowing she'd find Anamaria in the kitchen making bread and pasta for the luncheon they were hosting today.

But she didn't expect anyone else, so she paused at the doorway of the oversized stonewalled room when she spied several family members gathered around the giant table. They were sipping coffee, eating flaky biscuits, and deep in a serious and unusually soft-spoken conversation in Italian. Why weren't they working? In the vineyards or down in the cellar?

Even Bruno was there, and not even hung over, though he had gone out after dinner the night before.

"*Buongiorno.*" As she greeted them all, she couldn't help noticing that the conversation ceased instantly when they saw her. "Pre-event meeting without me?" she asked, always using English as they'd requested. They all wanted to improve their English, because it was so good for tourism, which was one of the reasons they'd offered her the job in the first place. That and the fact that she flat out refused to leave.

Anamaria left a fluffy dough ball she was working on, giving Kyra a thick mug of strong coffee. "You no sleep," the old woman whispered. "I hear you in the night."

"Then neither did you." She leaned closer and let her

cheek brush the crinkly one Anamaria offered, thanking her. "*Grazie mille,* Nonna."

She took the coffee to the table, sliding onto the bench next to Sofia. "What is going on here?" Kyra asked, sensing the tension.

Sofia rubbed her massive baby belly. Antonio looked down at his food. Lorenzo shrugged, silent. Filippa refolded her napkin and looked around the table.

"Is something wrong?" Kyra asked.

No one answered, and that just ratcheted that tension higher.

"It's about…him," Lorenzo finally said.

She didn't need an explanation to know who "him" was. She scooted closer to the table, wanting to reassure them. "Look, I took the liberty of inviting *him* to the event today."

"He will come?" Antonio asked, his arm protectively around the back of Sofia's chair.

"He hasn't answered." At least not in the last fifteen seconds, since she'd checked her phone three hundred times since she'd sent the text. Maybe she'd gone too far with the emojis. He probably wasn't an emoji kind of guy. *Maybe, Kyra?*

"The manager contacted me this morning," Lorenzo said. "William Hayward."

"This morning?" Kyra did the math on the time difference between Italy and New York. "They must work round the clock."

Lorenzo sighed and rubbed his temples. He didn't look like he'd slept any better than she had, considering the shadows under his dark eyes and the furrow in his brow. In his fifties, Lorenzo was still a handsome man, but the weight of the entire family always seemed to bow his broad shoulders.

Never more than right now.

"*Buongiorno*." At the sound of Elena's voice from the hall, Lorenzo dropped his hands, a smile in his eyes as his wife's soothing effect became immediately visible.

Their oldest son, Enzo, was right behind her as they came into the kitchen, each carrying a stack of papers. "I found what I could," Enzo said.

"It's not enough," Elena said, sitting next to Lorenzo but looking at Kyra. "We don't have what he wants." Her English was the best in the whole family, and she used it often.

"Which is what?" Kyra asked.

Elena's sage-green gaze dimmed with worry. "The business manager sent us…demands, I think is the word."

"What kind of demands?"

Lorenzo and Elena exchanged a look, one of a thousand that passed between them in a day, indecipherable to anyone but the two of them.

"Stupid demands!" Bruno exclaimed, his hot Italian temper always just under the surface and ready to bubble up. "No owner comes for twenty-four years, and now? We must bow and scrape to this man and find things we not have?"

Elena quieted her volatile son with a raised hand. "These are not the usual things that the business manager sees, not the inventory receipts or…normal spreadsheets. Other things."

Enzo handed Kyra a piece of paper from the top of his stack, and instantly, she noticed the computer printout was in English. Was that the problem? They couldn't read it?

"Okay," Kyra said after a quick perusal. "He wants a

description of liens, a discretionary earnings and cash flow statement, supplier and distribution contracts, an asset depreciation schedule..." She stopped reading, though there was more. "This might as well be in Italian," she muttered. "Or Chinese. I can translate, but I'm not sure I can tell you what these things are."

"We know a few," Elena said. "But we do not run the business so...official, you know?"

"I have some." Enzo tapped his papers. "But not all."

"Why does he want this now?" Kyra asked.

No one answered, but they all looked worried enough to make Kyra think they knew but weren't saying.

"So he can cook the books," Bruno murmured. "That's why."

"What you mean 'cook books'?" Anamaria demanded. "Who cook paper?"

Kyra waved off the question and Bruno's ridiculous assertions. "James is a very thorough businessman. And you must create annual reports and provide statements of profit and loss, right? You owe that to the owners, don't you?" she asked.

"Some," Lorenzo said, gazing at the list again. When he looked up, the lines that furrowed his brow deepened. "But we worry about the wine, Kyra. The harvest, the production, the quality. Some bookkeeping, of course, but...not...*asset depreciation*, whatever that is."

She wasn't entirely sure, but she sensed that a well-run company would track that. This family wasn't worried about money. They wanted wines that won awards for pride. James Brannigan might not understand that pride. Hell, he didn't even drink wine and probably didn't know a precious *rosato* from cheap white zinfandel.

"He just wants a complete picture of the business,"

she said, not really understanding her need to defend him. "You don't have anything to hide, right? The winery is profitable, *sì*?"

"*Sì, sì*." Lorenzo nodded. "The tourism has four times improved in the last year," he said, pointing at her. "It's your fault."

She smiled at the misuse of the language, but got the gist. "I'm glad. And you have nothing to worry about. Maybe he just wants to invest and build the business even more."

"Why?" Bruno asked. "His father never added to the business. He just let it run like—like we didn't matter. Of course, we don't to people like that."

She shot him a dismissive look. "The father is not the son," Kyra insisted. "He's young and smart and successful. He knows a good thing when he sees it, and yesterday, he saw it." She beamed at them, willing her optimism to reach their hearts. "This is great news, I think."

None of them looked like they thought it was great news.

"We must know…" Anamaria put a floury hand on Kyra's shoulder and added some pressure, proving again that her ability to follow an English conversation was excellent. "What he is gonna do."

For a long moment, none of them spoke, but the three of them shared more silent side-eyes that made Kyra willing to bet her last paycheck that they'd already talked about this and come up with a plan.

And the way they were looking at her…

"What? You want me to ask him?"

"Not ask," Elena said. "But make him tell you."

"Make him?" She choked softly. "Torture the truth out of him?"

And again with the shared looks.

"The opposite of that," Elena said softly.

Kyra inched back, eyes widening, gripping the table for a little support. "Are you suggesting I…" She couldn't even say what she thought they were suggesting.

"No!" Lorenzo exclaimed.

"*Naturalmente no!*" Elena added.

"Absolutely not!" Sofia and Antonio insisted.

And then they all got real quiet.

"Then what?" Kyra directed the question to Elena, who had to have the most sense and the best command of the language, and Kyra needed a clear answer.

"If he cares for you, he might tell you the truth. He will tell you the truth. And then we will know what his plans for us are."

She tried to respond to that, but it just came out as a little whimper of disbelief.

"Maka the boy trust you, *Cara*," Anamaria said, using the Italian nickname the family had given her since they'd never heard the name Kyra until she arrived. Usually, the word for "dear" softened her heart and made her feel like she truly belonged here, but right now, she was too bewildered by what they were asking her to do.

"And then break his confidence?"

"For *la famiglia*," Lorenzo said, putting his hand over hers again. "*La famiglia è tutto.*"

Oh, he was bringing out the big guns now, using the late patriarch Giorgio's favorite saying. The one that hung on a tapestry in the dining room and that was embroidered into pillows in the living room as well as the fabric of this household. *La famiglia è tutto*…the family is everything.

And it was, she thought with a resigned sigh.

This family. Her great big adopted Italian family. The family she never had but dreamed of her whole life. She'd wandered into their winery on a lark a year and a half ago, and they'd given her a home, a job, and a seat at the table, and a place in their hearts.

How could she say no when they were so scared to lose their livelihoods? Their home? This family couldn't break. She wouldn't let it.

"Okay, let me get this straight. You want me to get, uh, cozy with the new owner and find out his plans for our winery."

Anamaria came closer, frowning suddenly. "What is this 'cozy'?"

"Close. Comfortable." She wrapped her arms around herself to mime a hug. "Cozy."

"*Sì, sì,*" Anamaria said. "Cozy. Not..." She bent her arms and pumped her round hips in and out.

"Mamma!" Lorenzo barked.

The old woman grinned her yellowed smile. "Only cozy." She rubbed her own arms sweetly.

Kyra turned to Elena, praying for some common sense, but the motherly person in the group was smiling and nodding.

"You think this is smart?" Kyra asked. "And...ethical?"

"*Cara, Cara,*" she whispered. "We just want to know what he will do with our business. Then we can plan and adjust. With the boys and the baby and Nonna..."

Kyra sighed. Of course. This winery was their life and future. They needed to know what he was planning to do. She could find that out, right?

"Maybe," she said. "I mean, I could try."

If only he'd answer her texts. She picked up her

phone to check again, just as Nico and Gianni came flying into the kitchen, breathless and vibrating with news.

"Brannigan!" Nico exclaimed.

"He's come back!" Gianni added.

Kyra inched back in surprise, catching the smug look of satisfaction on Anamaria's face.

"Quello era facile," the old lady muttered.

Yes, that *was* easy, Kyra mentally agreed. But making James trust her and tell her his plans for a business might not be.

"Take him to town," Elena said suddenly.

Town? "He hates my scooter."

"Take Bruno's car," Lorenzo suggested, nudging his son. "Give her the keys."

"Why can't he be here?" Kyra asked.

"We're getting ready for the lunch," Elena told her. "You go be alone. Walk through town. To the beach. It is beautiful, and you'll be…cozy."

She stood slowly, nodding. No one could walk the beach in Positano and not fall in love. With the *beach*. "Okay, Operation Cozy, here we go."

They all grinned at her like accomplices. And she looked from one dear face to the next and knew why she would do just about anything to help these people. Even get cozy with James Brannigan.

Not that it would exactly hurt.

Chapter Eight

Taking the Eden Roc shuttle bus up to the winery hadn't been as exhilarating—or terrifying—as the motor scooter, but it hadn't been exactly relaxing, either. Still, James arrived in one piece, cool, calm, and collected. Despite his interrupted sleep, he'd risen rested, and dressed in linen pants and a cotton shirt before enjoying a bountiful breakfast at the hotel.

It was time to get back to business.

Climbing out of the shuttle at the gate to the winery, he was ready to review the documents he'd requested and then adjust the price and make some real money on this place. Which, he'd decided upon waking, was exactly the reason Colin gave it to him. Nothing more mysterious, nefarious, or life-altering than that.

Hayward had balked, of course, at the idea of increasing the price in the middle of negotiations and adding a mountain of documentation to justify the new amount. But since he worked for James, he'd given in and sent the request. So now James wanted to read that paperwork and nothing else.

No wine drinking. No grape eating. No bocce playing. No...*fun*.

But as soon as the shuttle left, he caught sight of two

little rascals scurrying down from a giant tree and running to the house to announce his arrival. He couldn't help smiling at the boys and admiring their clever and secretive lookout over the vineyards and the road leading up to their home. It reminded him of the tree house at the ranch, a place to spy and hide and enjoy the hell out of their young lives.

How lucky they were, he mused. Tamping down an unexpected ache for his own lost childhood, James yanked open the gate. As he did, a flash of yellow caught his eye. He peered through the flower-covered trellis, half expecting the urchins to come tear-assing back to climb all over him.

But the yellow didn't belong to a little boy. No, indeed. *That* was no little boy. That was one helluva beautiful woman in a dress the very color of the juicy lemons that hung from every other tree on the Amalfi Coast. Somehow both sweet and sexy, the dress fit her curves and still left a little to the imagination.

So much for all that hard-won control.

She walked toward him, her wild mane ruffled by the breeze, her body moving with just enough purpose to make him think her imagination might have been overactive last night, too. His mouth went a little dry, no doubt because of the blaring sunshine. In fact, his whole body felt abnormally overheated.

"Well, this is a pleasant surprise," she called out, shielding her eyes from the sun. "I was waiting for a text and I get the man himself."

He felt the nudge of guilt for not texting her, but buried it. "I've come to review the documents my business manager asked for."

"Oh, that." She flicked her hand as if his meeting were nothing but an annoying gnat on a summer day. "I don't think Lorenzo made it to the bottom of the email before his eyes glazed over and he ran for the closest bottle of *rosso*." She let out a lilt of a laugh when she got closer and reached for the gate. "He'll need days to pull all that together."

"Days?" James gave a soft snort. "I don't have days."

"At least a week." She unlatched the wrought-iron bolt and opened the gate slowly with the sweetest smile, like she was opening the gates of heaven and inviting him in. But she stepped out before he could get inside, slyly keeping him out.

"I can't stay here for a week. Why would it take so long?"

"Because you're in Italy." She looked up at him, momentarily blinding him with those damn dimples. He'd forgotten those in his imagination last night. He'd been too focused on her cascade of blond curls and the slight rise of her breasts when she took a breath or let out one of her musical laughs.

Get a grip, James. "There are no files, computers, calculators, or spreadsheets in Italy?"

And there was the laugh, like a wind chime. "There is no *speed* in Italy. Only on the road, not in business. Here, we savor every moment. We live, eat, drink, and make love quite slowly."

She gazed up at him, all innocence and light, all charming and disarming, like she hadn't just slipped that *make love* bombshell into the middle of a casual conversation.

Did this blond bomb-dropper think he was born yesterday? Did she think he could be swayed by dimples and cleavage and big blue eyes and sideways references to sex?

"In my business, nothing is slow," he replied, even

colder than he needed to be in an act of sheer self-preservation. "I asked for information and expect to get it. Promptly."

She made a face, squishing her nose and somehow becoming even more adorable than when she was smiling. Damn it. He never liked adorable women. He liked statuesque, cool, sleek women. Not…*lemon drops*.

"Sorry," she said, as if apologizing for being so appealing. "But that information? Not happening today."

"Why not?" He let his distaste for the news come out loud and clear in the question.

"Because he has to find it and prepare it for you."

"Nothing I've asked for should be hard to find. Not for a well-run business, anyway."

She shrugged off the implication. "But I told you what's happening today. A large American group has booked the winery for a tour and late afternoon tasting and luncheon. There are travel agents in the group, and we have to impress them. Honestly, James, they take precedence over…*documents*."

"Not to me."

"Sorry, but the whole house is working this morning, and you just can't go in there now and turn things upside down to suit your schedule."

Irritation skittered up his spine. "Except it's *my* winery and *my* schedule."

Her expression grew serious. "Then you should want nothing more than for the winery to run well and make money. Interrupting what's happening in there is counterproductive to what you want for your business and your schedule." She crossed her arms with a playful, nonverbal *so there*, and if she wasn't so damn *precious*, he'd march right by her and get what he wanted.

Instead, he stood staring at her like an idiot. "When?"

"When is the tasting and luncheon? Not for a few hours. Would you like to go to town and shop? You haven't lived until you've shopped in Positano."

He snorted. "No, I would not like to go to town and shop. I'm here to work, not shop."

"But we could have *granita al limone*, right on the beach. And wait until you see the porcelain and jewelry and so much leather. It's beautiful!" She clapped her hands like she always did after a breathy exclamation. "Come on, I'll take you there."

"On that motor scooter again? I don't think so."

She rolled her eyes. "Bruno has a small car I'll borrow if you're scared."

"I'm not scared."

She lifted a dubious brow.

"I am *not* scared," he reiterated. "I am, however, the owner of a rather large business, and this is just one of many holdings and interests that demand my attention. I don't have time to go riding around on a motor scooter shopping for porcelain."

She sighed. "Okay, suit yourself. But you aren't meeting with Lorenzo today, and that's that. So goodbye, then." She backed up, slipping back behind the gate and reaching to close it *in his face*.

"I hope you've arranged a way back down the mountain," she added with a playful smile. "Because it would be very hot and tiring to walk."

"Just a second." He grabbed the latch before it snapped. "I need to see Lorenzo."

"You can," she assured him. "At the tour, tasting, and luncheon. I've saved you a seat." She smiled. "Next to me."

He started to argue, then caught himself. What was wrong with him? He should be exploiting this advantage, not fighting it. Hadn't his father taught him that in all business dealings? He could practically hear Colin's voice now. *Use what's given to you and make it work for you, not against you.*

He could learn a lot about the business by watching them in action with a group. It could help him demand a higher price. And it wouldn't kill him to have lunch next to her. She could tell him the ins and outs of the family, and he'd be able to share that with the new owners. But first, he'd get more information out of her and if that had to be on a shopping trip, fine.

James put his hand over hers on the gate. "You win, lemondrop."

She inched back, surprised by the sudden change of heart. "I do?"

"Yep. Town, shopping, lunch with the tourists, whatever the schedule, we'll do it your way. Nice and slow."

A soft flush rose on her cheeks, making her even prettier. "Okay." Her voice cracked...as if he'd called her bluff. "Let's go."

The tourists had already invaded in full force, so the town of Positano was hot and crowded and a little chaotic. Kyra decided that just added to its charm, but James seemed to keep an invisible wall around himself as they threaded through the crowds and trotted down the legendary stone stairs called the *scalinatella*.

She explained that the long, winding path and steps that snaked through the town and led to the beach were the subject of countless Italian folk songs, and he seemed fascinated by that but still more of an observer than a participant.

He asked questions, mostly. Some as they'd descended the mountain by car, parked with the valet at the Eden Roc, and then more as they continued on foot. He'd asked about the town, the seasonal nature of the tourism, the best restaurants and hotels. Small talk, but plenty of it.

All along the *scalinatella* down to the beach, he slowed to check the storefronts and stopped to look over the rooftops draped in carpets of bougainvillea, gazing at the cobalt water of the Mediterranean. But not like someone falling for the exquisite beauty of Positano. More like an art expert examining a piece to determine its value.

Did the man have no soul?

"Isn't it pretty?" she asked, a little worried how he might answer.

A smile curved the corner of his lips, and the hard line of his jaw softened under the dark shadow of whiskers he hadn't shaved off this morning. "Pretty...full of tourists."

"Well, it's early May, and the season is officially in full swing. But you can see beyond that, right?"

"Tourists are good for the business," he said simply.

Of course. That's what mattered to him. Not the history, flavor, color, or charm of this picturesque town.

"Positano is the most incredible place on earth," she said solemnly, as if telling him would sway him. "And I say that with the confidence of a person who has had her feet on every continent and some of the most remote places in the world."

He turned, studying her, analyzing this information like all the rest. "So, were you serious when you said you came for a visit and never left?" He started walking again, this time toward the pergola-covered stairs that led to the heart of the city—a pedestrian-only warren of tiled walkways lined with festive shops and shaded by flowers and fronds.

"Yep," she replied. "And in about two months, it will be the longest I've ever lived at the same address."

"Really?" He paused and lifted his sunglasses to search her face as if the statement was so preposterous he might catch her in a lie. But it was no lie.

"I lived in San Francisco when I was nine for twenty-one months and six days. I'm going to beat that for sure."

"Why did you move so much? Parents in the military or something?"

Before she could answer, a pack of tourists came right at them, forcing James and Kyra to pick a side. He took her hand and guided her to the right, around the people.

The move was natural, keeping them from separating, but sent an *unnatural* thrill through her. His hand was strong, large, a little rougher than she'd expect from a pampered executive, and she didn't want to let go.

Apparently, neither did he, since they still held hands when the tourists passed and they were alone on the wide stone stairs again. Probably so they wouldn't lose each other in the crowds.

But that didn't make it feel any less intimate.

"Not the military and just one parent, my mother," Kyra finally answered. "She was a business consultant who essentially was sent from company to company to work for a year, then move to another. We never lived anywhere more than a year or so."

He frowned a little. "That can't have been a very stable upbringing."

"I had wonderful nannies," she said, not bothering to hide the sarcasm. "But no home. At least, no single place I called home."

"Did you like that?"

"I never knew any other life. We lived very well but very…temporary. My mother was a workaholic with a huge job that came with a lot of stress." They lingered in front of a high wall of painted trays outside a ceramic shop, but instead of the bold colors and smooth porcelain famous up and down the Amalfi Coast, Kyra saw her mother. "She was a closer. Do you know what that is?"

"Yes, I do." He gave a dry laugh as they took a step into the open-air entrance of the store. "She went into companies to shut them down and fire people?"

"Of course you know what that is."

"I use closers all the time," he said, reaching to run a finger along a yellow and blue bowl painted with lemons and grapes.

He did? Used them for…*what*?

Despite the merciless May heat, a chill danced up her spine. Was that why he'd come to Villa Pietro? To *close* it? And then the Sebastianis would be like all of those people crushed by the stroke of her mother's pen.

"Would you like it?" he asked.

To see her beloved family lose the winery? "No."

He inched back, the bowl in his hand. "Oh, okay. I thought…" He put the bowl down. "I thought you wanted to shop, and I wanted to get it for you."

Her heart tugged a little at the unexpected kindness. "Why?"

He seemed a little perplexed by that, looking at the tray, then her. "I guess it reminds me of you, lemondrop."

She felt her cheeks warm as she looked up at him, studying his face as he did the same thing to her.

The chatter of tourists around them was suddenly drowned out by the unexpected thump of her pulse, and the scents of citrus soap and fresh basil from the pizzeria nearby drifted away. All the colors of Positano faded as she looked directly into bottomless brown eyes that pinned her to one place.

And for that one crazy moment, all Kyra could think of was how much she wanted to kiss him.

"Lemons," she managed, "are the official symbol of the Amalfi Coast. You have to taste the *granita*. Would you like some?"

"You know what?" He put a warm hand on her bare shoulder, his fingers strong and steady and masculine enough for her to feel a response to that touch right down to her toes. "I would like some. Very much."

"Okay." But something told her he wasn't talking about *granita*.

Chapter Nine

For the next hour or two, James never looked at his watch, and time did something it never did for him. It melted away. If forgetting about time, appointments, cares, and business was the magic of Positano, then the place had powers indeed.

But looking at the woman next to him, mesmerized by the dusting of freckles across the bridge of her nose and the six different shades of gold and honey in her hair, James knew the truth.

Positano wasn't magic. But Kyra Summers was doing a little bewitching of her own, and with every minute they spent in the sun, time wasn't the only thing melting. So was his determination to view this excursion as an extension of his business, examining the tourist-trap town as a line item that would increase the value of his property.

She laughed, and he did, too. She shared something, and he would, too. She took his hand, and he refused to let go, and the next thing he knew, he was sitting on a stone wall—not a table or bench, a *wall*—side by side with a charming woman, facing the sea, watching the promenade of bathing-suit-clad tourists in front of them.

And he really didn't want to be anywhere else on earth in that moment.

"And then," she said, her eyes dancing as she lifted a spoonful of the frozen ice to punctuate the punch line of her story. "Anamaria just stood there with her hands in her apron pockets and stared at the guy until he gave her every last olive in the bin."

He laughed with her, digging at the tangy treat in a paper cup with his own plastic spoon, as mesmerized by the tales of the Sebastiani family as he was with the woman spinning them. "Anamaria always gets what she wants, I take it?"

"Always," Kyra assured him. "And when she wanted me?" She put her hand on her chest as if she simply couldn't keep her heart where it belonged. "Best moment of my life."

He set the cup next to him, turning a little to get a better look at her. "How did that happen, exactly?"

He told himself that her story would help him understand this new property he owned, but the truth was he adored watching her talk. He loved the way her feminine hands flitted to underscore every point, like everyone who talked in this country, and how her cornflower-blue eyes mirrored her humor and lit up her whole face. If someone took this colorful, charming, seductive little town and turned it into a person, it would be Kyra Summers.

Couldn't put her as a line item on a property value statement, though.

"Well, I told you I went for a tour of the winery," she said, oblivious to his musings. "I was spending a few months just in Italy. Started way north in the lakes"—she used the spoon to point up on an imaginary map—"then in Milan, then a month in Florence, which was amazing." Her spoon traveled as she had. "I moved down to Rome, where my Italian got really good when I had a job in a restaurant called Piccolo Arancio near the Trevi Fountain. Best food in Rome. Possibly the world."

She paused to taste the *granita*, giving him a chance to watch her close her eyes in silent appreciation of the burst of flavor and her memories of a job at a restaurant. She really had lived everywhere and never stayed anywhere. It was fascinating to him. *She* was fascinating to him.

"Anyway, I hadn't ever been down here to southern Italy, and I just wanted to see it." She gestured toward the view beyond the restaurant patio where they sat. "I toured Villa Pietro and stayed all day until the family invited me for dinner."

"They just plucked you out of the tour line and said, 'Stay for dinner'?"

"Bruno did, actually."

"Ahh, that makes sense." Bruno, the quiet one who stared at James and drank a lot of wine.

"No, no." She waved a finger at him. "Everyone thinks that because we're close in age and single, but there's no interest at all there. Zero. Bruno is like a brother to me, and a butt pain one at that, and frankly, the man is a little, you know…"

He frowned, shaking his head.

"Cah-razy." Her finger moved to her temple to circle around.

All the more reason to watch him, James thought.

"I drank so much wine and dinner went so late that Anamaria wanted me to stay in her little house, which I did. That night, I started teaching her some English, because she was dying to learn. She's so smart, James!" She grinned at him. "Honestly, the woman is a secret genius. And she was lonely out there in the cottage. There are two bedrooms and…" She lifted her shoulder. "One day led to another, then another, then I started helping them with the tours, and Anamaria and I became roommates."

"An unlikely pair, for sure."

She laughed, letting her head go back to reveal the silky column of her throat, which suddenly looked tastier than the dessert they ate. "Isn't that the truth? But I love her with my whole heart and soul."

She paused to take another bite, leaving James to wonder what it would be like when someone this luminescent loved with all she had. It would be…warm.

"I never had a grandmother," she continued. "Never had a mother, in truth, since mine worked eight days a week."

"I didn't have one, either," he said softly.

"Oh, James, of course." She put her cup and spoon down to reach for him. "Gah. I'm sorry to be so cavalier about mine, who was very much alive even if she wasn't around often." She added some pressure to his hand, her fingers so soft it nearly killed him not to lift them up and feel them against his lips. "What was she like? Do you remember her?"

He considered the question for a moment, realizing again how rarely he talked about Kathleen Brannigan. Her memory seemed to have faded among his brothers, and Dad almost never mentioned her name. If he had, there'd always been enough of a shadow of pain in his father's expression that James knew to avoid the subject.

He rarely thought about those twelve years in his childhood. They were before she died. All the years that followed, they were…after. It was a clear line in his life, and he rarely crossed it. But here in the sunshine, with a woman who had all that same vibrancy?

He took the step backward.

"I do remember her," he said. "At least with the eyes of a twelve-year-old." He turned from Kyra, his gaze settling on a jaunty orange umbrella on the beach. It was perky, cheery, a little off to one side, and bathed in light. That umbrella captured the essence of his mother.

He shifted his focus and realized with a jolt that it also captured Kyra Summers. "You remind me of her," he said, the admission surprising him, but as soon as he said it, he understood how true it was.

"I remind you of…your mother?"

He laughed at her uncertain reaction. "It's a compliment, believe me. The last time I saw her, she was young, and that's the only way I'll ever know her. Beautiful and lively."

"Ohhh." Her whole body softened, inching slightly closer as if that very warmth of hers could offer sympathy. "Tell me about her."

"She was…bright." It was the first word that came to his mind.

"I have no doubt your mother was smart," Kyra said.

"Yes, but that's not the kind of bright I mean. She was like light. Wherever she went, it was warmer and brighter and better." He was surprised at how tight his throat had become, picking up his ice water to wash down an unexpected kick of emotion.

"She sounds lovely."

He nodded as he swallowed. "She had a great sense of humor, too, which I guess kept her sane in a house with seven sons."

"It must have been awful."

"All those boys? Nah, it was just chaos most of the

time, a lot of roughhousing and noise, but…oh…" He read her expression and realized she meant when his mother died. "It was. The worst."

She searched his face, clearly wary of how much she should ask, yet she looked sympathetic and interested.

"She died in a car accident," he said quickly. "She was, uh, running an errand and got hit by a kid who just got his license."

"Oh." She put her hand over his. "How tragic."

"It was," he agreed. "Life as I knew it changed in an instant."

"The light went out," she said softly, the words damn near crumbling his heart in pieces. How did she get that? No one else did.

But then, had he ever shared this much with anyone else? About his mother? Unlikely.

He turned away, picking up the cup of melted ice next to him. "This was as good as you promised, by the way."

She smiled, obviously getting his clumsy subject change. "Next you have to try an aperol spritz. Oh, and the pizza. It's the best in the world, right over there in that little shack."

"Aren't we going to lunch at the winery?"

"Later this afternoon. Come on, let's keep walking. You have to put your feet in the Mediterranean or you haven't been to Positano."

He looked down at his linen pants. Casual, but not water-ready. "Not today."

"Then tomorrow." She stood and, still holding his hand, pulled him off the wall. "Or the next day."

"I'm not going to be here that long." But the minute the words were out, something told him they weren't true. At least, he didn't want them to be.

"But you can't go without swimming in the sea. Or seeing Ravello! Or Capri! You can't leave without seeing the Blue Grotto, remember? And it's just a short boat ride away." As they walked, she linked his arm and practically skipped during the litany of what they had to do in Positano.

"You're determined to make me have fun, aren't you?"

She grinned up at him, finally slowing down. "Yes, I am. I am the official arbiter of fun, and you are having it. Starting now."

He stopped them completely in the middle of the promenade, turning her to face him. "Why?"

She inched back. "Why have fun? Oh, James. Who even asks a question like that?"

He added a little pressure to her warm, smooth shoulders and narrowed his eyes. "Why is it so important to you that I have fun? Why not just let me do my business, stay holed up in my hotel, and go back to where I came from?"

He could have sworn she paled a little, almost as if she was hiding something, but just as quickly, her color returned as she bit her lip and declined to answer.

"Why, Kyra?"

"Because..."

He watched her throat move with a tight swallow and her smile falter. She *was* hiding something from him. Something about the winery? The family? The property he owned?

"I like you," she whispered.

Oh. He tipped his head, the answer so unexpected. "I like you, too."

A slow smile lifted the corners of her mouth and formed those insanely cute dimples. "Because I remind you of your mother?"

"No," he said. "Because you make me forget time and drink wine and sit on a wall eating Italian ice."

The dimples deepened. "Don't forget ride a motor scooter and the boat ride to Capri we're going to take and oh, that double-decker rooftop bus ride up to Ravello will be one for the books. Just you wait and see how much fun is in store."

So much time with her could only lead to... Well, *that* would be nice. Very nice.

"Is that it, then?" He eased her a centimeter closer. "Is that all the fun you have planned?"

"Ummm..." She slipped that pink lip under her front tooth and bit hard enough to make him wonder if it hurt. And what it tasted like. He really wanted to know.

"Or do you have anything else fun planned, lemondrop?"

She held his gaze for a good long moment, the sun blasting so hard he thought they'd both melt right into the promenade. And then she stood on her tiptoes and gave him the lightest, sweetest, airiest, fastest kiss that ever sparked on his lips.

"Just that," she whispered.

"Okay," he said. "I'll stay for a few days."

That made her laugh. That precious musical laugh that he swore he'd hear in his sleep tonight. Or maybe just in his bed.

At least he hoped so.

Chapter Ten

"*Cara, Cara!*" Elena came rushing into the kitchen on Kyra's heels the very first time they had a minute to be alone. "We must talk. Lorenzo? *Dov'è Lorenzo?*"

"I saw Lorenzo in the pantry with Nonna," Kyra said, knowing they'd pounce on her now. The afternoon had slid into evening with very few opportunities for Kyra to talk to anyone privately. For one thing, James stayed close to her, using her translation capabilities as an excuse for being by her side, and the occasional brush of their hands or shoulders. Not a very good excuse, since many of the guests were Americans.

"*Vieni, vieni!*" Elena ordered her to come with her, pulling Kyra toward the walk-in storage area in the back of the kitchen. As soon as she did, Anamaria and Lorenzo stopped talking.

"What you learn from him?" Anamaria demanded.

She sighed, knowing she hadn't done her job in terms of getting a drop of insight into his plans. Yes, she'd done exactly what the family had asked her to do—cozy up to their new owner to find out what his plans were. Well, she'd cozied, all right. Spent a dreamy day in town, lingered over another of Antonio's spectacular tasting, enjoyed a luncheon al fresco with delicious food and now Anamaria's tastiest desserts.

But the three eldest and most concerned in the family waited for her, huddled in the pantry, expecting news.

What could she tell them? That when James laughed and relaxed, she found him to be flat-out irresistible? So irresistible that she'd pecked him on the lips right in the middle of the beach? And that he'd agreed to stay...because of that very strong mutual attraction?

Yes, that's what they needed to know. "He is staying a few days," she said, entering the walk-in pantry where the familiar scents of herbs and flour mixed with their obvious sense of worry.

"Good, good," Anamaria mumbled, her hand deep in her apron, fiddling with whatever she kept in those pockets today—peanuts, garlic cloves, or a rosary.

"But why is he here? What is his plan?" Lorenzo asked.

"What did you learn about his business?" Elena added.

That he used a closer when he shut down companies and ruined people's lives, like her mother did. She shoved that thought away, not willing to scare them like that yet.

"I'm taking it slow," she said. "If I push too hard, he won't show his hand."

Anamaria's brows drew together. "Why would he hide a hand?"

Kyra shook her head, remembering how Anamaria struggled with idioms. "He won't tell me everything. That's not how businesses like his work."

No, they swoop in, take over, hand out pink slips like candy. How many times had she heard her mother on the phone, reporting into the home office, detailing head count...heads *chopped off* count. Jane Summers was cold and calculating, in every imaginable way.

Kyra would slip into her mother's bed late at night, desperate for her company and willing to settle for listening to half of a boring business discussion just to be with her, aching for someone who wasn't a nanny or tutor or housekeeper or stranger.

She'd learned a lot during those one-sided calls. She didn't know it when she was young, but as she got older and realized what her mother was talking about, she understood. And, slowly, she'd taken the other side and learned to despise people who had no soul, who didn't think about the little guy, who wrecked lives and careers for the sake of the almighty bottom line.

Was that who James Brannigan was?

"He seems very calm," Lorenzo said, crossing his arms to look from one woman to the next. "Better than yesterday."

"Because of Kyra." Elena put a hand on Kyra's shoulder. "You are charming him."

"That's what you wanted me to do, right?"

"Not too much charming," Anamaria warned. "If he's like his father." She tsked and shook her head. "All the time with the bedroom."

"They were married," Lorenzo said. "He is not...bedrooming with Kyra."

She rolled her eyes at the word, but not the idea. *Bedrooming* with James wouldn't be horrible. But it would be taking *cozy* to a new and tricky level. "I have to spend time with him for him to trust me enough to tell me what he's planning to do. And Lorenzo, you *have* to supply the documents he asked for."

Lorenzo let out a sigh and shared a look with Elena.

"He's your boss," Kyra reminded him.

But they were silent.

"What is it? Is there a problem getting him what he wants?" she asked.

"We can get it," Elena said. "But not everything is quite right yet."

Kyra felt her brows draw together, sensing there was something major they weren't telling her. "What exactly does that mean?"

"Nothing, nothing," Lorenzo assured her. "We simply must have all the, how do you say, chickens lined up."

"Ducks in a row," she said slowly, looking from one to the other. "Do you?"

"Most ducks," Elena assured her. "Still this…this 'asset depreciation schedule' and distribution contracts. Why does he need to know which trucking companies we use, Kyra? Is it that important?"

Kyra stifled a sigh, once more thinking of her mother and those calls. She'd heard of an asset depreciation schedule and knew exactly why third-party contracts mattered…to someone who was decimating a business. And a family.

"It's important to him," she said, refusing to let her optimism be cut in half. That couldn't be what he was going to do. "I'll buy some more time with him, but you need to get what you can, Lorenzo. I'll tell him he'll get it tomorrow. Can you do that?"

He gave a classic Lorenzo shrug.

"*Tu lo farai!*" Anamaria ordered with a light whack on his shoulder.

"*Sì, Mamma. I will do it.*"

"Go, *Cara*." Anamaria gave her a much gentler nudge. "Go and cozy more and more."

As if she needed to be ordered to get cozier. She was

already fantasizing about another kiss—a real one. Kyra stepped out of the pantry, smack into Bruno, who had obviously been out there waiting for her.

"I do not like him, Kyra."

She felt her shoulders sag. Why was everyone's opinion of this man *her* problem? "You don't have to, Bruno."

His dark eyes narrowed, surprisingly clear, making Kyra realize she'd never seen him have so much as a sip of wine today. "I Google him."

"We all did," she assured him. "We know that he runs a billion-dollar hedge fund called Brannigan Capital Management Group, lives in New York City, is the oldest of seven, got his undergrad and business degrees from Stanford University, owns a private plane and, now, a vineyard."

"And the women."

Yes, she'd seen those pictures, too. James Brannigan with a South American model at a fundraiser. James Brannigan with the daughter of an Indonesian billionaire. James Brannigan with a woman who had no job but surely worked as an Angelina Jolie impersonator in her spare time. "What about them?" she asked, hearing the defiant edge in her voice.

"You are…different."

She choked softly. "You mean I'm out of my league, in over my head, and not his type? Do you forget that this is just a way for one of us to get 'cozy' and find out what his plans are for the winery?"

"Did you?" he countered.

She wanted to scream with annoyance. "Not yet."

"Be careful," he said. "I no trust him."

"In what way?"

He sighed with the same force and fear that Lorenzo had.

"Bruno," she urged. "What do you mean you don't trust him?"

He leaned closer. "He's stealing from the winery."

Her eyes popped. "That's preposterous, Bruno. He owns it."

"I know what I know."

"Which means what?"

He heaved a breath at the sound of footsteps. "He's stealing from the company and is going to put it on my shoulders, that's what I think."

"You're crazy." She glanced at the door, knowing someone had to be close. "He's a rich man. Why would he—"

"Kyra, are you in here?" James called from just outside the kitchen.

Bruno lifted an eyebrow. "Don't worry. I'll fix it," he said angrily. "I'll fix—"

"There you are." James walked into the kitchen, holding a glass of red wine, wearing an expression that never failed to spark something in Kyra's chest. Yes, he was a handsome man when he was chilling out with the family, forgetting business and drinking wine. "Antonio has sent me to the cellar to find the 2011 Rosso Riserva," he said. "I think it's a test, and I don't like to fail. Will you help me?"

"Of course." She turned to Bruno. "Unless you'd like to take him down to the cellars? You know your way around a bottle of Riserva."

Bruno just closed his eyes and shook his head. Then, to James, "I can take you back to your hotel whenever you're ready."

Kyra shot him a look. "James is in no hurry to get home."

"But when I do," James said. "I intend to leave with

the paperwork I've requested. Maybe your time is better spent helping your brother pull that together, Bruno."

Bruno visibly bristled at the order, but held it together to nod, pivot, and leave the kitchen.

Just then, the pantry door opened and out poured Anamaria, Lorenzo, and Elena, still nattering in Italian.

James looked surprised, but Kyra gestured to the door. "Come to the cellars with me, James. I'll show you the wine vault."

"*Sì, sì.*" Anamaria beamed at them. "The cellars are…cozy."

Cozy and cold.

But James relished the break from the heat of the outdoors and a chance to be alone with Kyra again. The same thing happened at this party that had plagued him in town. He tried to participate in the role of the current owner of the winery, and next thing he knew, he had a bocce ball in one hand and a glass of wine in the other. Work became fun.

How did she do that?

Now, his hands were empty and itching to touch the woman who continued to weave a spell around him. He used the cold as an excuse to put an arm around her as she led him deeper into a maze of tunnel-like cellars lined with hundreds of oak barrels, all marked with wine names and dates.

"It's always a little chilly down here," she said, but didn't make any move to step away from him. In fact, he could have sworn she tucked herself a little closer to him and shivered just a little. "But it has to be in order to age the wine properly."

JAMES

"The vineyards and pergolas are amazing," James said, reaching out a hand to touch the rough limestone wall and marvel at the fact that the cellars were built right into the mountain. "But I have to say, I've never seen anything quite like this cellar."

"You only saw part of it yesterday, where Antonio holds the preliminary tasting and as far as we let tourists in. But now, you're in for a real treat."

"This whole day has been a real treat," he admitted as they turned a corner into another long barrel-lined corridor.

"Well, listen to Mr. James 'I Have to Work' Brannigan."

"Don't remind me. I don't even want to read email or look at my missed calls when I get back to the hotel."

"What exactly do you do, anyway? Or is that a rude question?"

"Not at all. I run a hedge fund."

"Which could mean you plant bushes, for all I know."

He laughed. "Not that kind of hedge. Although, that's where the term came from—hedging your bets. It's a tricky form of financial risk management, but to make it easy to understand, I carefully move money from one place to another and make more of it."

"Is money important to you?"

He slowed his step a bit, not expecting a question quite that personal or deep. "I like having it," he said. "And I like making it," he added, not caring if that sounded shallow because he wasn't the least bit ashamed of that. "Mostly, I enjoy the challenge of finding a good investment, the test of my nerves when I make a big one, and the happiness on my client's face when they see their statement."

"Hmm." She nodded and gestured to a door built into the stone. "This is the secret stash."

But her non-reaction bothered him. "What does that mean, *hmm*?"

"Nothing, just…" She stopped at the door and put her hand on the oversized knob. "I'm not generally a fan of the person who chases the almighty dollar. I watched what it did to my mother and didn't like it."

"What did it do to your mother?"

She gave a slight shrug. "I don't think you can love money and people at the same time."

"How can you say that? I know plenty of wealthy people who love their family and spouses."

"Yeah, well, sure. But at some point, you have to make a choice."

"My dad had money and he…" He couldn't finish the sentence, because the truth would probably help make her point.

Her expression said she knew just that. "He what?" she urged.

"Well, it's true he wasn't home much, and when he was, he wasn't exactly involved in our lives. I gave him reports. But before my mother died? He was all in. He loved her and loved that big brood of his. I don't blame money on his distance. I blame grief."

"I'm sure it was difficult." She opened the door, and a long squeak echoed through the limestone corridor as she guided him into a darkened room. "But what about you? Do you…love anyone?"

"I have a big family, and I love them all."

"Do you?"

The challenge irked a little. "I do. Not like this family, obviously. We don't see each other much, but they mean a lot to me."

"And what about *someone* in particular?" He heard her swallow like the question was hard to ask. Or she was scared of the answer.

Oh, so *that's* where she was going.

He shot a slow smile at her, less aware of the hundreds of bottles in stacks around him, the dusty smell, or the heavy silence as she waited for the answer. "Why are you asking, Kyra?"

"Never mind. Not my business." She gestured around. "Welcome to the vault. Family only, so consider yourself lucky. Take a sniff."

He did, his nose filling again with a musky, earthy scent that reminded him of the red wine. The floor was dirt, not tile like outside, and it was as cold as a refrigerator in here.

"I love that smell," she said, rubbing her bare arms for warmth, then reaching up to pull a string and shed a thin ray of light from a low-watt bulb.

"That's it?" He looked up at the crude fixture.

"Light messes with the wines and the temperature, so it's dark and cold. I'll use my phone flashlight to find the 2011 Rosso Riserva." She inhaled again and took a look around. "I think the first time I stepped in this room was when I fell in love with the wine. Like you say, the vineyards are spectacular and the views out there can't be beat, but there's something special about how it all goes from that to..." She ran a finger along a dusty row of bottle tops. "This."

He glanced at the stacks, then back to her. "I didn't answer your question about someone *particular* in my life."

"That's fine. I've seen pictures to know enough about your social life."

That made him laugh softly. "You have?"

"Well, obviously, when we found out you were the new owner and coming here, I, well, we...looked you up." She averted her gaze again, suddenly very interested in the wine bottles. "Now where would we find the Rosso Riserva? I think it's back here."

She rounded a large stack, and he followed, deep into the bowels of the wine cellar now, where another few hundred bottles created eight-foot-high walls on either side of them.

"What kind of pictures tell you about my social life?" he asked.

"Pictures with women." She pulled out a bottle, turned it, and put it back, though he couldn't imagine how she'd read the label in the dim light.

"That sounds compromising."

She finally met his gaze. "Nothing bad, I assure you. But let's be honest. You do have a type."

Yes, he had. Past tense. "You think?"

She turned to the stacks, her back to him, and pulled out another bottle. "Long, lean, dark, and mean."

"The women or that wine?"

That made her shoulders move with a quick laugh. "Both. It's normal. Like people either want light, crisp white or bold, deep red. You obviously like them...bold."

He stepped closer, looking at the wines over her head. "That's a pretty big assumption to make from a quick Internet search of a few fundraisers I've been to."

"More than a few," she said. "Fundraisers and women."

Placing a light hand on her shoulder, he gently turned her around. "More fundraisers than women, which is to say, no, there is no one special. Please don't turn that into an indictment of my values or my love affair with the almighty dollar. I'm single, that's it. Are you?"

The question made her eyes widen a little. "Yes." It was little more than a whisper, but the lone syllable sounded good. "But based on what I see, I'm not your type."

On the contrary. "I don't have a type."

"Hah. You haven't Googled yourself lately."

"No, I sure haven't." His gaze dropped from her eyes to her mouth, that lower lip damp from her teeth and luscious. "But you can't believe everything you see on the Internet, lemondrop, don't you know that?"

"I know what I saw, and they were all...beautiful."

"You're beautiful."

She closed her eyes, and the dimples deepened. "You're flirting with me."

"Ya think?"

"Why are you doing that?" she asked.

"Maybe you've been out of the country too long."

She frowned a bit. "Not following."

"Because in my country, the United States of America..." He trailed a single finger over her bare shoulder, certain that the chill bumps he felt weren't just from the room temperature. "It's cultural protocol to flirt just a little bit before..."

"Before?" The question was just breathless enough to urge him on.

"Before the first kiss."

She exhaled softly. "But...we've had our first kiss. Remember the peck on the beach?"

"Actually..." He inched closer, and she couldn't move back without hitting the expensive wine bottles. "I can't forget it."

She held his gaze, her chest rising and falling with each breath. "It wasn't that unforgettable."

"But it was bold, and I believe you've mentioned that as part of my 'type,' right?"

"And dark and exotic and…modely."

"Modely?" He smiled and shook his head. "Today, my type is blond and blue-eyed and…bubbly." He lowered his head just an inch from hers. "And this kiss?"

"Mmmm?"

"Will be unforgettable."

He eased her closer and met her halfway, placing his lips on hers lightly at first, then adding pressure. She stilled for a moment, then relaxed a little, kissing him back with exactly the enthusiasm he'd expect from her.

She tasted as sweet as the wine, and just as intoxicating. Sliding his hand down her arm for the sheer pleasure of touching more silky skin, he angled his head and ventured deeper, letting their tongues touch for the first time.

The first and not last time, he knew.

A soft whimper caught in her throat, the sound so feminine and sexy, he drew her closer, wrapping his arm around her waist and enjoying the feel of her hands working up his arms and shoulders and finally locking behind his neck.

Her lips were parted and willing, and then…gone. She leaned back but didn't let go of him, her eyes still closed, a dreamy expression on her face.

"Oh," she said on a soft breath. "Definitely unforgettable."

"And definitely…" He cupped her cheek and stroked that smooth skin again. "My type."

"You're lying, but that kiss was worth it."

He brushed the pad of his thumb against her lower lip, not willing to let go of that precious part of her yet. "All right, you win. I probably never have taken a blonde to a fundraiser. But everything's different here, isn't it?"

"In Italy?" She smiled. "I told you it's magical."

"I want more." His voice was gruff, but he wasn't going to hide how he felt. One kiss wasn't enough. Not nearly enough.

"More Italy?" Her eyes held a tease.

"If that means more of you."

She shuddered slightly in his arms. "Okay. Tomorrow, I'll take you to Ravello. Or Capri. Or the beach. Wherever you want to go."

He wanted to go to bed with her, now. His blood was heated, his body tense, his whole lower half tightening as arousal pumped through him. Everything in him wanted to kiss her again, to push her against the bottle stacks and get under that dress and see if every inch of Kyra Summers was as warm and seductive as her personality.

Somehow, he dug for control, loosening his grip.

"Tour guide's choice," he managed to say. "I'm all yours for whatever you want."

"I want..." She finally separated and stepped away. "To get back upstairs before we're gone too long and half the Sebastiani family comes looking for me."

"Then get the wine, Kyra," he reminded her.

"Oh yes, the wine." She gave a breathless sigh, glancing around. "What were we sent to get again?"

"A 2011 Rosso Riserva." He smiled. "Did I fluster you with that kiss?"

"Fluster?" She tapped her chest as if proving she could breathe just fine. "No, no, you didn't." She reached over her shoulder, pulled a random bottle of wine, and blew the dust off the label. "The *rossos* are right here, and I don't fluster that easily, Jimmy."

He snorted. "Jimmy?"

"If you can call me lemondrop, I can call you Jimmy."

"No. You can't."

"Even when we're alone?"

He angled his head toward the door. "If that's what it takes to be alone with you, then…maybe. Actually, no. Call me James."

She just laughed, the music of it echoing over cellar walls and hitting somewhere tender in his heart. Truth was, she could call him anything she wanted as long as it meant they would be alone again soon.

Chapter Eleven

After the long day of sun, food, wine, and one very memorable kiss in the wine cellars, James had a hard time concentrating on work that night. But it was still the middle of the business day in the States, so he did his best to dig through emails and messages and finally settled into the comfortable couch with the documentation he'd gotten from Lorenzo Sebastiani.

It had come with a litany of caveats, promises for more, and pleas for a chance to go over everything together—at least that was what Kyra relayed when she translated for them—but James wanted to read everything himself. Surely William Hayward had all of this already, since it was critical information for putting together the sale, but...

His heart sank a little at the thought of selling the winery. Obviously, it was the intelligent business decision. A sale would give him cash that he could reinvest in something with bigger and faster profits. He wasn't in the wine business; he was in the investment business, and that's how he made money.

Hayward knew that, and that's why he was able to find the perfect buyer—another winery looking to expand into Italy. Once James approved the final numbers, it was just a matter of negotiating the highest price possible.

This was simple. This was his job. This was...

Not right.

The words hit his gut with a little too much force. He didn't understand why this one—oh hell. He understood. Two days and evenings, some tours and tastings, a lot of food and family and, yes, fun. All topped off by one extremely alluring and surprisingly persuasive little package of sunshine, and he was ready to reconsider this winery. Ready to lose money. Ready to most likely make a mistake, which was exceedingly rare in life or business for James Brannigan.

He stared out the open balcony doors, watching clouds drift in front of the moon, his mind going back to that moment when his father made this decision.

And the question: Why?

Did any of his brothers have the answer? He'd tried Gabe, and the one clear-thinking business-minded brother he trusted most had babbled about *things you can't put a price on*. Damn.

Who could make sense out of this? He was also close to Finn, but he had his hands and life full these days. Only James knew that his youngest brother had been in a plane that was shot down over Afghanistan a few months ago and that Finn had quietly ended his career in the Navy. He wasn't the brother to be a sounding board now. Not about this.

Knox was on his way to Yosemite to see Luke, from what Gabe had told him. That left Hunter, who bugged the shit out of James most of the time, and Max.

Of course, Max. He hadn't done a damn thing about his inheritance, but basically had ignored it for as long as he could, heading off to another overseas mission before even opening the envelope.

When he had, Max discovered Dad had given him an aging horse farm in Kentucky, and when James talked to him last month, his brother had been trying to figure out what the hell to do with it. A woman had put the farm up as collateral for a loan, and Max had gone to call it in and, in James's opinion, stood to make a handsome profit.

Which he should have done by now, at least if Max followed the advice James had given him.

Without knowing what continent he might find his brother, James tapped his contact screen and made the call, a little surprised when Max answered on the first ring, his voice low, clear, and calm. "James. Good to hear from you, my man." At least it didn't sound like he was in some obscure country protecting the world.

"How are you, Max?" James asked. They weren't close, but they didn't go head to head like James did with Knox and Hunter. Max was always cool, a trait that served him well when he was in Special Ops, kicking ass and taking names.

"Really good. How goes the world of high finance?"

If only he could remember. "Running without me for a few days," he replied. "I'm in Italy checking on that winery Dad decided to pawn off on me."

Max laughed. "I don't think he was 'pawning off' anything. And I'm sure it's easy on the eyes over there."

He closed those eyes and thought of Kyra. "Very easy," he agreed. "So, did you get the horse farm on the market? I wouldn't mind a little recon on how that went for you, since I'm in the same boat with my legacy."

"Yeah, well..." Max gave a little chuckle. "It didn't exactly go as planned."

"Really? Well, you'll find a buyer. Shouldn't take much time. How often do you have to go back to Kentucky?"

"Actually, I'm still here."

James drew back, blinking in surprise. "That's like six weeks, man. You must be writhing in agony and anxious to get back into the field. How's that security firm even running without you?"

"Pretty well since I quit."

"Seriously?"

Max lived for his career as a contract soldier, a mercenary who took risks to save lives the way other men breathed. He quit to…to do what? "Are you living in Kentucky?" It was so preposterous, he couldn't quite get the words out.

Max just laughed again, in a way that gave James the impression he'd been asked this question before. "I am," he confirmed. "And I have more news, big brother. I'm engaged."

"Holy shit." James dropped back on his chair. "They're dropping like flies in this family."

"I know last time we talked we were mocking those brothers of ours, and you, me and Finn had it all figured out, but…"

James waited for this explanation because it had to be rich.

"But, bro, once you find it, the whole world changes."

No, the world hadn't changed. Max had. "Then I'm happy for you."

"You don't sound happy."

"I'm shocked, Max. I'm…" He huffed out a breath and tapped the speaker icon so he could put the phone down and pace the expanse of the living room.

JAMES

"You're what?"

Scared. Curious. Starting to think there was more to these legacies than…money. "Nothing, just blown away by the news. And really happy for you, man. Seriously. Tell me about her. Who is this woman? What kind of witchcraft did it take to bag a man who lives on the hairy edge and then saddle him up in Kentucky? Pun intended."

"Ellie? She's amazing, James. Never knew a woman like her. She's warm and funny and, damn, you should see her ride a saddlebred horse. It's a thing of beauty, I tell you.

And she takes no shit from nobody."

James scratched his head, listening, a smile pulling. "That's great, Max. And one of these days I'll have to jet into Kentucky. They have runways there?" he teased.

"I'll let you know when we set a date, and you better be here."

"I will," he promised.

"So, what the hell are you going to do with that winery? Besides send cases of the good stuff to us?"

"I'm not sure," he said honestly. "I mean, I have an offer on the table that I haven't even started to negotiate yet because I wanted to see the place, but…"

"But now you're wondering why Dad did what he did, aren't you?"

He sure as hell was. "It does seem like there was some method to the old man's madness." He tunneled his fingers into his hair, closing his eyes. "Although, I really would like to be wrong about that."

"Why?"

"Because it's one thing to be manipulated, but when a dead guy's pulling the strings? It pisses me off."

"He isn't manipulating anyone or anything," Max

said firmly. "But, for me? This experience has changed everything, and for the better. Give it all a chance to work on you."

He didn't want anything working on him. "Yeah, sure," he said vaguely. "I better go. You give my best to...Ellie? That's her name?"

"Elinor, actually. You're going to love her, James. I sure do."

"I'm glad."

They talked for a few more minutes, but when he hung up and picked up the papers from the winery, Max's words echoed in James's head. Was it possible, likely even, that Colin Brannigan had made his legacy decisions quite strategically?

If so, what did he want James to find out about this winery?

He shuffled through a discretionary earnings and cash flow statement. Although they called it something else in Italian, he recognized a P&L in any language. He noticed the name of a distributor and frowned, not remembering an American distributor in the supplier and distribution contracts. He found that original document, scanned it, and didn't see that American company. He saw a similar name for shipments to New York, but the two lists didn't match.

He texted Hayward to see if he'd caught the discrepancy, and even that little act of management made him feel better and closer to what mattered. Making money.

Is money important to you, James?

He tried to silence the echo of a question he didn't like being asked as his thumb hovered over the phone screen. But before he signed off, he added one more sentence...

JAMES

How committed are we to this deal, in your opinion?

He stared at the question, imagined Hayward's eyes popping out behind his brainy accountant's specs, then hit send.

The response came back in seconds.

We can't back out now. Don't even think about it.

But, deep inside, James was thinking about it.

Kyra took the stairs up to Suite 6 at the Eden Roc the next morning, stopping in front of the door to catch her breath and slow her heart rate. But not because she was winded. All morning, she'd been a little breathless in anticipation of seeing James.

In fact, since she'd said good-bye to him about twelve hours ago, she hadn't thought about anything else but that secret, sexy kiss in the wine vault and how much she wanted another one. And another. And…*oh*.

This could get complicated. It was one thing trying to discern his plans for the winery by getting friendly and taking him around the sights of Amalfi. It was something else completely to fall into his arms and give in to the chemistry that was crackling between them.

He was, in essence, her boss. And he was, in essence, a hardened, cold, calculating executive who held the fates of the winery and people she loved in his hands. And she was, in essence, achingly attracted to him.

Forget essence. In *reality*, this was all too complicated.

Well, she wasn't going to climb into the sack with him today, that was for sure. It was a day in Ravello to visit the iconic Villa Rufolo or a boat trip to Capri and the famed Blue Grotto. There shouldn't be any kissing. Not too much, anyway.

She tapped on the door and waited a moment, hearing James's voice as he came to let her in. He was speaking in low, serious tones, pausing between sentences, obviously on the phone.

When he opened the door, a phone to his ear, his dark eyes widened, and he smiled at the sight of her. And her heart flopped around like a helpless fish out of water. This shouldn't feel like a date. This shouldn't feel like *this*.

But it did.

He gave her cheek the most casual brush with his fingertip and winked his greeting, the whole gesture taking no more than a millisecond, and yet it made her feel a little weak and giddy.

Come on, Kyra. Get a grip.

He held up a finger to say he'd be only a minute, then turned it to point her to the living room, all the while talking brusquely about an accrual swap, whatever the heck that was. On her way, she stole a look at a new style for James—khaki shorts, a loose-fitting white T-shirt, bare feet, and damp hair like he'd just gotten out of the shower.

She sucked in a breath trying not to react to that, and when he looked at her, she pretended it was just a response to the beautifully appointed living area and the expansive balcony beyond. She'd heard the Eden Roc was one of the best, if not the very best, boutique hotels in all of the Amalfi Coast, but she'd never been in one of the suites before.

She crossed cool, white marble, taking in the elegant rattan and linen furniture and original paintings on the walls. But the real beauty was the picture-perfect view beyond a wrought-iron and bougainvillea-trimmed balcony.

JAMES

Walking through the open French doors, she let him have some privacy to finish his call and leaned on the railing to drink in a vista that never got boring.

"That's not going to happen, Mr. Cheng," James said, his harsh tone conflicting with the casual clothes and damp hair. He could have been sitting at the head of a conference table in a three-piece suit, barking orders.

She imagined him like that, and all the fiery chemistry disappeared. She could never care for a man who lived that life. She could never care for a man with a cold heart. She turned for a moment to look at him. Was his heart cold? She really didn't know. Wherever they went today, it was her goal to find that out, too.

"I've promised my client enhanced indexing to amplify the returns of their entire portfolio," he continued. "And if you don't go along with that strategy, Brannigan Capital will take our business elsewhere and close your fund."

That was cold.

She had no idea what he was talking about, but it didn't take an MBA to hear the subtext of what he was saying: *I'm in charge, you'll do it my way, or we will squash you.*

An old ache crept up her chest, and despite the view, she closed her eyes and drifted back through time and space, hearing that same tone in her mother's voice on the phone with a client or her employer. Kyra loathed the iciness of business, which was why she'd lived her life in a way that avoided it and why Villa Pietro had sung a siren song when she arrived.

Warm people, warm sunshine, warm life. If a dollar was made, great. But if a person smiled or a couple kissed or a glass was filled with liquid joy, all the better.

Really, nothing explained her attraction to James,

other than the way he looked. And laughed. And kissed. And—

"So sorry." His arms wrapped around her waist from behind, pulling her into a hard, sizable chest. "Had to finish with Beijing." He kissed the top of her head, and Kyra swore she was going to lose her balance and tumble right over the balcony, down, down, down to the Mediterranean Sea.

"It's all right." Her voice came out tight, so she cleared her throat and turned in his arms. He didn't let go, letting their bodies slide against each other in a way that made things even more difficult. "Are you ready to go sightseeing?" she asked brightly when she looked up at him.

His smile faltered as he looked at her, really scrutinized her face, from eyes to mouth and back again. "I like the sights I'm seeing," he said softly.

About a thousand butterflies took flight in her stomach, ignoring every protest from her brain. "But I promised you Capri or Ravello. You can't do both in one day, but we should get going if we want to grab a tour boat and get on our way. We can go to the town of Amalfi and take the bus up to Ravello, or the funicular train in Capri—"

He put two fingers on her lips to quiet her. "I don't do tour boats or buses or, holy hell, funicular trains. Can't we stay here?"

"And…" Do what? "Hang out at the pool? Go to the beach? Walk into town again?" Her voice rose with each question, and surely he sensed her hesitation to just stay…in this room. Near his bed. In these arms that still held her just a little too tight.

"We can go sightseeing tomorrow," he said. "This place is beautiful, and I'm perfectly happy not getting into any form of a vehicle, boat, train, or scooter."

JAMES

Tomorrow. She felt a little wave of relief that he wasn't leaving just yet. "Well, Capri *is* a whole long day. In fact, it could take two to do it right."

"Stay over?" he asked, a devilish brow lifting. "Now that idea has merit."

She let out a soft laugh. "James," she whispered. "What are you doing?"

"If you need to ask, I'm not doing it very well." He brushed some hair off her face, the move intimate and sexy and touching. "I just want to be with you."

"That's not fun."

He added a little pressure. "What *is* this 'fun' you speak of?" he joked.

"What kind of person doesn't 'do' fun, anyway? And then admits it?"

"A person who…" He thought for a moment. "I was going to say a person who likes to maintain control, but blowing off a day to be with you, no matter what we do, isn't very controlled."

She studied him for a moment, lost in his dark eyes. "Why do you need to be in control?"

"Because I always am," he said simply.

"Don't you want to let go once in a while?"

"I've been letting go since I walked into this hotel, careened on a scooter up a mountain, drank a barrel of wine, and kissed my tour guide in the vault. This whole trip has been one big loss of control for me."

A slow smile pulled at her lips. "So what's one more ride up a mountain on the top of a double-decker bus with no roof?"

He laughed. "Besides insane?"

"Or we could take a boat under a rock and into a cave to see the Blue Grotto. The water is incandescent."

"*You* are incandescent."

A blush warmed her cheeks. "*You* are a flirt. And, by the way, you own the winery where I work. So I call that a conflict of interest."

"Or a brilliant career move."

She shook her head, still laughing. "I'm not going to win this."

"It's not a battle, lemondrop. It's…what was that word you used? Oh, I remember. *Fun*." He grinned at her, shifting his hands to cup her face. "This is fun."

She sighed. "Yeah, it is."

"Can we stay here, then?"

If she stayed in this hotel, she'd be a goner. In that bed before the end of the day. "Nope, we're going sightseeing today. And tomorrow. And maybe the next day."

He started to argue, then let his broad shoulders sag. "I'm all yours."

If only he was, she thought.

Chapter Twelve

Time stopped melting. Now it froze. The days passed, but for James, time seemed to stand still. He'd never gone so many days—and nights—without working. He barely looked at his phone and hadn't turned on his laptop. Just hours and hours of walking, boating, laughing, talking, taking pictures, and seeing so much beauty, it made him ache. And that was just looking at his tour guide.

At night, after long, late, delicious dinners, Kyra left his hotel, and he fell asleep, exhausted and happy.

Of course, he'd have been happier if she'd stayed. If their good-night kisses turned into overnight kisses, but something stopped them both. He wasn't entirely sure what was stopping her, but as long as that Whitehouse Wineries offer was open and on the table, he couldn't take her to bed. But that didn't stop him from holding her close, from kissing her and sliding his hands up and down her body, and making out with her like they were teenagers, until they were panting and weak.

She always managed to slip away, with plans for the next day of travel, leaving him alone and feeling like the sucker who continued to agree to one more night with Scheherazade just to get to the end of the story.

Before going to bed, he'd stare long and hard at that Whitehouse offer on the desk, almost ready to text Hayward and kill the deal, but something stopped him from doing that, too.

He'd told his business manager he was looking things over and then let everything hang, while he was paralyzed in Positano. Not in control. Not making a profit. Not doing anything but, at the moment, sitting by the Eden Roc rooftop pool with the brightest, most charming, and sexiest woman he could imagine.

What the hell was he doing?

"So this must be what a vacation is," he mused out loud.

On a chaise next to him, Kyra laughed. "Yes, James. This is what a vacation is."

"But you're taking one, too."

"Oh, I'm working," she assured him. "I'm here on behalf of Villa Pietro." She grinned. "Guest liaison."

"I'm not a guest," he said, his voice slightly tight as the pressure of his decision—and the fact that he hadn't even told her he had the decision to make—weighed more on his shoulders.

"But you are having fun." Kyra turned her head on the chaise, shielding her eyes even though she wore sunglasses.

"Are you?" he asked.

"Of course, although I really wanted to take you to the Duomo di Sant'Andrea today."

"I didn't want to go to a church."

She snorted. "It's so not 'a church,' but this is okay. Especially when you do things the Brannigan way."

He grinned at her, lifting his own sunglasses a bit because he didn't like anything impeding his view of her body in that bathing suit. "I didn't want anyone else around."

"So you paid the hotel for the exclusive use of the pool for the entire day."

He shrugged. "Private, isn't it?"

"And you sent the concierge to town to buy me an overpriced bathing suit when I could have had someone from the winery drive one down to me."

"Worth every penny." He took a long, lazy look, not even trying to hide the fact that he was staring at luscious curves, tanned skin, long legs, and the cutest little pink-tipped toes he could ever remember seeing. "Yellow is definitely your color."

She crossed her legs, fighting a smile as she trailed a finger over the lace trim of the bikini bottom. "I do like this suit. Thank you, again."

"No need. The pleasure is all mine." So much pleasure.

"I forgot how easy money makes things," she said, picking up an icy glass of Pellegrino water and moving the straw over the bouncing lime slice. "It used to make me mad that my mother threw money at everything."

He eyed her, hearing the sincerity and definite disgust in her voice. They'd talked a lot in the last few days, but both of them had managed to keep things from getting too personal. Lots of laughter, lots of tourist chatting, but he wanted more of her. Not just her body, but her background, too.

"Just an armchair psychologist's guess here," he said. "But I'm thinking it wasn't the money-throwing that made you mad."

She sighed. "You're right. It was just...her."

"Where was your father?" he asked.

"Is," she corrected. "He's alive and well and living in Marietta, Georgia, with his wife, three kids—who are now grown and reproducing at an alarming rate—plus two dogs and a turtle named Gomer, who somehow makes it on the Christmas card picture every year."

She tried to hide the bitterness in her voice with a healthy sip of water, but James heard it. "Because Gomer is on the Christmas card and not you?" he surmised.

"I'm on the Christmas card *list*, so there is that." She put the water down. "My parents divorced when I was three, and my dad remarried when I was still little, and his new family became his entire life. I went to visit a few weeks in the summer or Christmas now and again, but..." She shook her head. "No hard feelings. Just no feelings. My dad's life is in another world and with another family. I was always so jealous of them, but I never fit in there."

She dropped back, the hurt clear in her voice. "Oh how I wanted that family to be mine, James. But I was the outsider, not unwelcome, but not part of it, either. So it was just me, my mom, and a host of help who changed with every new town we moved to."

The bitterness left her voice, replaced by a hint of sadness that both touched and intrigued him. "Must have been hard to make friends if you moved a lot."

She grinned at him. "What are these friends you speak of?"

He laughed at the echo of his own joke. "If that's true, then you do realize that I don't have fun and you don't have friends, so that makes us a pretty pathetic pair."

"I have friends now," she assured him.

"Your best friend is an eighty-one-year-old woman who stands about four feet tall."

"Four foot nine inches of opinion and fire. Couldn't imagine a better friend," she said. "But I'm also close to

Sofia and Filippa. All of them, really. I've made friends in my own travels, all over the globe."

"Fifty countries," he said, remembering her story.

"But none like here."

"I'd think after all that moving around as a kid, you'd want to settle in one place."

"I have," she said. "But it took traveling to fifty countries to find this."

"I suppose you talk to your mother a lot, though," he said, a little surprised at how much he wanted to know the details of her life.

"Not really," she said, shifting a little as if the conversation made her uncomfortable. "She doesn't do 'close,' as you would say. Ever meet a person who has sort of a plexiglass wall around them? You can see them, but you can't quite touch them? That's my mother, which, I suppose, was her defense mechanism for her horrible job of having to fire people and close companies."

He knew exactly how horrible that job could be, which was why he hired closers himself when he needed to have that done.

"Have you ever known anyone like that?" she asked.

"My dad," he replied, knowing he had to give personal information if he was expecting to get it. "He wasn't always that way, but after my mother died, yeah. Plexiglass wall. Perfect description. I was able to get behind it more often than my brothers, probably because I was the oldest, and when I became an adult, I followed a similar business path, so we had more in common."

She pushed her sunglasses back on her head, listening intently, a question in her eyes.

"What?" he asked her.

"I'm just wondering...why."

"Why we had so much in common?"

"Why he willed you this winery that he never came to after he bought it. I understand all of you got something, but I assume the gifting wasn't random."

He gave a dry smile. "So the woman is beautiful *and* smart."

"Thanks, but am I right?"

He turned a little, ignoring the view for the pleasure of having someone to discuss the very question that had plagued him for so long. "One would assume that Colin knew what he was doing, but none of us has any clue what it was."

"Even after they, what did you call it, *dealt* with their legacies?"

He sighed. "I don't know, since they've all changed so much since he died."

"How?" she asked.

"Well, for one thing, five of them either got engaged or married."

"Really? Just in the past, what, eight or nine months?"

"My theory is that my father must have been holding them back from relationships, because they fell like dominoes after he died." He shook his head, still in shock at what had transpired among the Brannigan men and the conversation he'd had with Max the other night. "Only Finn is left, but he's recently left the Navy after some really tough tours in Afghanistan, and now he's going to Alaska to figure out why Dad left him a small airline with three planes."

"And you're here, trying to figure out the same thing." She blew out a breath that sounded a lot like relief. "Well, that's good news."

"Why?"

"Because if you're just trying to learn that, then you're not, you know, messing with the winery."

He swallowed and hoped she didn't notice his reaction to the statement. Messing with the winery? Like…selling it? Yeah, that would be messing. But something kept him from telling her his plans. *Something*, like he knew damn well she wouldn't like it—or him—once he made that public.

There'd be no more fun with Kyra. The realization hit him like a punch in the gut. He was withholding the truth from her so he could be with her, which wasn't cool. Not at all.

He wasn't sleeping with her…yet.

"Do you have any theories on why he left it to you?" she asked.

"He knows I appreciate…" A good real estate deal and wise investments. "Wine."

She snorted. "You don't even drink it."

"I do now, apparently."

Reaching toward him, she put her fingers on his arm, the touch warm and intimate. "Maybe he left it to you because it's the most beautiful place on earth and he loved you and wants you to have something that is precious and wonderful."

"Precious and wonderful," he echoed. "Not sure those things were high on my father's list of values. He was more about money."

She rolled her eyes. "Now, that I get."

"So, I assume he thought I would want this winery for…" It was his turn to shift in his seat. "Profit," he finished. "It makes a profit."

Enough for him to sell it, anyway. He took a breath. He really should tell—

"James, I can help you!" she exclaimed, sitting up.

"Make a profit?"

She flicked her hand as if to rid the conversation of anything as ridiculous as a *profit*. "Anamaria spent so much time with your parents when they were here," she said excitedly. "She might know the answer to why he sent you here."

He didn't *send* James here. He gave him the winery as a gift, an inheritance. To do whatever he wanted with, not because it was some kind of scavenger hunt for the past.

"I know it was a long time ago," she continued, "but Anamaria has a memory like a steel trap. She remembers details from when she was a child living here. Maybe she remembers something about them."

"Other than they spent their time trying to make an eighth baby?"

"But don't you see? That's the kind of thing she knows. Let's talk to her. I'll help you, because her English isn't great. Or would you just like me to talk to her, if it, you know, is too difficult to talk about your mother?"

He looked at her for a long time, knowing he was staring and trying to process about a hundred different emotions that were completely foreign to him. He went with the only one that felt normal.

"God, you're beautiful."

"James."

"No, really, you're gorgeous and…" *Oh man.* "Good. You have a good heart, Kyra."

She slid her fingers down his arm to curl them around his hand. "Let's go talk to her."

"Now?"

"Why not? Don't you want to know?"

Not as much as he wanted to lie in the sun and look at that yellow bikini. And then take it off.

JAMES

And *then* tell her he was planning to sell the winery.

Wrong on every level. Once he found out the why of Dad's gift, then maybe he wouldn't sell it. Or he would. He didn't know, but he sure as hell wasn't going to sleep with her while that unspoken fact hung between them. So going to Villa Pietro and talking to Anamaria made sense. It was a logical part of a business plan that might dictate his next move.

And Kyra was already standing up. "She'll be getting up from her afternoon nap. We'll talk to her, and then we can—"

"Stop." He reached up and took her hand, pulling her back toward his chaise, reluctant to end this perfect taste of a vacation. "I reserved this pool and patio for a private party of two."

She buckled and let her bottom drop next to him, her skin warm against his. His whole body reacted, tight and needy. "You can unreserve it."

"Kyra." His voice was husky as he pulled her down to him. "We can go on this errand and find out this stuff, which, I have to tell you, isn't pleasant or fun for me, but then..." Tunneling his fingers into her hair, he guided her face to his, letting his kiss finish the sentence.

She pressed against him, hot, slick skin and sweet, sexy curves, opening her mouth to take his tongue and moan as the kiss grew deeper.

He stroked her back, sliding his hand over the slope of her spine then over the sweet slope of her backside. She rocked against him in response, and instantly he grew hard, a state he'd been learning to live in for days. And nights. And was damn sick of it.

"We can talk to Anamaria later," she murmured into the kiss, sucking in a breath when his thumb dipped into the bikini bottom and grazed more skin. "Tonight."

It would be easy to take her up to his suite now and do what they were both dying to do. Easy and...*fun*.

"James?" She lifted away from him, expecting a response.

"Let's go now. I want to get it over with."

"Get it over with?" Slowly, she sat up, searching his face. "You don't really want to talk about your mother, do you?"

"Oh, let's see. Talk about my mother, or take that bathing suit off with my teeth?" Sitting up, he put his hands on her shoulders and let them slide an inch or two closer to her breasts, not caring that his erection had to be obvious in his board shorts. "Which do you think I want to do?"

She just closed her eyes and smiled. "You'll do what's right, I think."

"Always. Let's go."

"On the scooter?"

He looked skyward. "Let the good times roll, lemondrop."

"They will, I promise."

He took one more kiss. "Good, because I can't wait much longer."

Chapter Thirteen

In spite of the fun and relaxation—and increasingly smokin'-hot make-out sessions—they'd shared, James was still taut with nerves when they rode Kyra's scooter up the mountain. He was quiet as she wended through the twists and turns, except for when he swore mightily at one particularly hairy near miss with a lost tourist who should never have been allowed to rent a car.

At least it meant he held tight to Kyra, his hands strong around her waist, his legs pressed against her, his breath warm on her shoulder and neck. Every time they had to lean into the next turn, he literally braced for death.

He didn't relax until they reached the winery, parked her bike, and took one of the paths through the vineyard.

"We really have to get you to drive this sometime," she said as they walked. "It will show you how much control the driver has."

He snorted. "None. At least not over the other guy."

She gave up the discussion when the small stone cottage she called home came into view.

"It's humble," she said as they got closer, imagining what her frill-free existence looked like to someone who lived in a penthouse apartment in New York and jetted around in his own plane.

The outer walls were the same gray and cream limestone as the surrounding hills, with a simple wooden door that led into a common room that was kitchen, living, and dining all in one. Two bedrooms and one shared bath were off the main room, plus a loft they rarely used. She knew when they walked inside that the main room would smell like garlic and baked bread, cooled by slate floors and wide-open windows.

Once inside, those windows would let in the clean and citrusy Amalfi breeze and the sounds of the workers in the vineyards. But it was home, and she loved it.

"Nonna," Kyra called as she opened the door and peeked in.

Anamaria was at the sink, rinsing dishes. She turned, beaming at the sight of Kyra. "*Buongiorno, Cara.*"

"James is with me," Kyra said right away, gesturing for him to come in.

Anamaria's brows rose. "No Duomo today?"

Kyra shook her head as they entered. "Maybe tomorrow," she said in Italian.

"English," Anamaria corrected, wiping her hands on her ever-present apron as she came forward, smiling up at James. The difference in his six-feet-plus height and her four-nine was laughable, but that didn't stop Anamaria from dropping her head back to meet his gaze with that fearless, spirited streak that Kyra had grown to love so much.

"With you and James, I speak English." Anamaria pulled out a chair for him and ordered him into it with a pointed finger.

"We had lunch, Nonna," Kyra said, knowing the woman's first instinct would be to feed them.

JAMES

"Then we do the after lunch," she said, leaving no room for argument as James took a seat at the scarred, wooden table. Almost immediately, Anamaria produced her jug of Pietro table wine, which was as close to homemade wine as this Italian winery family would ever have.

She added three thick juice glasses, and next came a tray of the amaretto butter cookies she'd baked yesterday, followed by a nudge to James's shoulder, ordering him to *mangia*.

He sneaked a smile at Kyra and poured them each a glass of wine.

"Why you no go to Duomo Sant'Andrea?" Anamaria asked as she sat down and pushed the tray of cookies to him. "Is beautiful."

"We took a day off from sightseeing," he said, lifting his glass in a toast. "And we wanted to visit with you."

Anamaria's dark eyes flashed, and the slightest color rose in her cheeks, proving that no woman on earth was entirely immune to his charms. "Me?"

James glanced at Kyra again, as if to give her a chance to explain this errand.

"Nonna," she said. "James was wondering if you remember anything about the time his parents were here. Any details, any information at all about their vacation."

Anamaria nodded slowly. "Oh, *sì*. Very much remembering. They were *speciali* even before I knew *Signor* Brannigan would be the one in control of us."

"He was hardly in control," James mused. "What else can you tell me? Other than the fact that they spent a lot of time in their..." He frowned. "Did they stay in the main house?"

"They stay right here," she said, sweeping a hand to indicate the room around them. "Back in that day,

Giorgio and I lived in the big house with Enzo and Antonio and used these cottages for guests. Not too many hotels in Positano like now."

He leaned back on his chair and let his gaze drift around as if trying to imagine his parents staying in a place like this. Very slowly, a smile lifted his lips.

"I can see that," he said. "She'd go for something like this. Rustic and authentic." His face changed when he talked about his mother, Kyra noticed. His features softened and his eyes warmed.

"Oh, she love the house," Anamaria confirmed. "She always have the fresh flowers every day all over." She took a cookie, lost in her thoughts for a moment. "I clean the rooms then," she said softly. "I talk to her and bring her flowers."

"She liked flowers," James confirmed, his gaze on Anamaria but distant enough that Kyra suspected he was digging around his memory banks. They must be dim after, what did he say? He was twelve when she died? Twenty-three years.

Kyra's heart slipped a little, hurting for that little boy and his six younger brothers, losing their happy, flower-loving mom.

"Anamaria, do you remember anything else?" James asked, leaning forward. "Do you have any idea why he decided to buy the winery?"

Dark brows drew together in an old Italian version of an *are you serious?* look. "Of course I know."

James sat up straighter, inhaling a little. "Can you tell me?"

She took a deep sip of her wine and looked hard at him, a silent request that he do the same.

He took a drink and set the glass down. "I would like to know," he finally said.

"*Sì, sì.* He talk to my husband, Giorgio, who tell him that *Signor* Casella, the owner who live in Rome, want to sell the winery. Giorgio tell *Signor* Brannigan that we are very scared. Like now. Very scared."

Kyra watched James's face for a reaction to that, but he gave nothing away. His gaze was intent on Anamaria, as if by looking at her he could draw out the answers he sought.

"My Giorgio tell *Signor* Brannigan all about it. They drink wine together and talk. *Signor* Brannigan say he would buy Pietro, then we no scared anymore. He said it would be..." She fluttered her hands, trying to describe something, then looked at Kyra. "*Una sorpresa per il suo compleanno.*"

"He wanted it to be a surprise for her birthday," Kyra translated.

A little color drained from his face. "Her birthday?" James frowned. "It was a birthday present?"

"*Sì, sì,*" Anamaria confirmed. "And he buy it after they leave, just like he said he would. *Signor* Casella come here and say good-bye and tell us *Signor* Brannigan bought property and we keep our homes and jobs." Her lips stretched over yellow teeth in a heartfelt smile. "We have a big party then. So much food. *In abbondanza!*"

James didn't smile back. "She died before her birthday that year," he said. "She died in February, and her birthday was in March."

Anamaria lifted her brows. "Your father, he love my Giorgio. They like this." She held up two fingers smashed together. "They drink and laugh, and Giorgio teach *Signor* Brannigan his favorite expression. *La famiglia è tutto!* All the time. *Signor* Brannigan, he love that."

When James looked at her, Kyra explained, "It means 'the family is everything.'"

"*La famiglia...*" He didn't finish the Italian, emotion crushing him enough that Kyra could see his shoulders sink.

"*La famiglia è tutto*," Anamaria repeated. "He tell his wife, your mother. They like those words. I guess with the big Brannigan *famiglia*."

James nodded very slowly. "She had a little jewelry box on her dresser that said that." He swallowed hard. "I'd completely forgotten it until now."

Anamaria made a squeal of joy, placing her hands over her mouth. "I send that to her for Christmas that year! So happy she would come back, but I kept the secret of her present. But then, months later..." Her joy evaporated with a sad sigh. "We learn she never come back. Do you have?"

"No, I don't have it," James said. "Somehow it got lost." He fell back into his chair, silent, making Kyra to literally ache for him. "Like a lot of things."

But Anamaria brightened, clasping her hands like Kyra did now when she had a great idea. "You should go to the tree. It make you happy," the older woman said.

He looked up, his focus sharp again. "What tree?"

"The big lemon tree. I found it years later, after they were gone. *Signor* Brannigan never come back. We wait and wait, but he never return. We get money, we get business man to visit, we make wine. No Brannigan. But once I was picking the lemons and I found the tree. *Their* tree." She leaned forward and looked at Kyra. "You take him to the lemon grove," she said, shifting into Italian. "The big tree in the middle, first one planted. You'll see."

JAMES

Kyra glanced at James to gauge his interest in a tree. "Yes?" she asked him.

"Maybe," he replied, pushing up to a stand. "*Grazie, Signora* Sebastiani," he said, reaching for her hand.

She glared at him. "Nonna," she corrected. "And you remember, James. Giorgio and *Signor* Brannigan drink the toast to Villa Pietro. He saved us. Your father, he saved us." She seized his hand and brought it to her lips. "*La famiglia è tutto*," she mumbled.

Anamaria looked tired, so they said their good-byes and walked out to the sunshine. There, James stared ahead at a vista she suspected he didn't see, silent.

"Do you want to go to the tree?" Kyra asked.

"And do what?"

"Let go of some of that pain?"

He smiled at her. "You are the single most optimistic person I've ever met."

She wrapped her arms around his waist and put her head on his chest, feeling his heart. "Maybe the second most optimistic," she said.

"Yeah, she was optimistic." He stroked her hair slowly. "Okay, lemondrop. Let's go see the tree."

James didn't know why Dad gave him the winery, but at least he knew why he bought it in the first place. And understood why he never returned or talked about it...or *sold* it.

Had he made a promise to Giorgio? Was James expected to keep that promise? That was exactly the opposite of what he planned to do.

"Right over here." Kyra led him to a thick-trunked tree in the center of the grove, standing taller than the rest. "It was the first tree in the grove that the Sebastiani family planted fifty years ago when they took over the care of the winery. Every year, they've planted another tree here, so there are fifty-two, I think. But this was first." She pointed to the tree, lifting her hand and gaze up to the mighty branches heavy with bright yellow fruit. More lemons were on the ground, too.

She got closer to the tree, examining the trunk, running her fingers over the bark. She looked up and smiled. "Oh. That's why she sent us here."

He followed her gaze and saw what Kyra did. Carved into the tree, inside a heart: *Colin loves Kathleen*.

Something that had existed as a wisp of a memory he rarely thought about suddenly sharpened into a clear and distinct image. The same words, in a heart, on another tree. "I've seen that," he said.

"But you've never been out here."

He stared at it, remembering when and where...and who. "It's on a tree in Yosemite, at the Algoma Resort. My brother Luke owns the place now, and lives there, but once, when we were kids, we were on vacation there, and my mom..." He swallowed hard, a little choked up at the unexpected impact of the memory.

He hadn't cried over her in twenty-three years. What the hell was wrong with him?

Kyra was silent, waiting while he cleared his throat to finish.

"My mom took me for a hike," he finally said. "Just me. No pesky brood following along. I might have been...ten? Pretty young. I don't remember the details, just that we were alone, because that was what was special." He could still see his young, happy, carefree mother as she held his hand and pointed to her tree with some long story about how Dad had carved that when they met at the resort as teenagers.

"Must have been unusual to be just the two of you in a family that big," Kyra said, staying close to him.

"Yeah, but she could do that, somehow. She could find ways to be alone with each of us even though there were so many. And when she did, it was…" His chest squeezed like his heart was in a vise grip.

"I bet it was nice," Kyra suggested.

"Better than nice. It was the best feeling in the world. When Mom focused all her energy on you, it was like…" He couldn't find a word without sounding ridiculous and like some lost little boy. "It was great."

"She must have been awesome," Kyra said, making his heart feel even more tender with her genuine sympathy.

"When we were alone, she always taught me something or made me laugh or…"

Son of a bitch, his eyes were tearing up.

"It's okay, James," Kyra said, taking his hand. "You're so lucky to have had someone who loved you like that. Even if it was only for twelve years. You were so, so lucky."

He nodded, digging for his composure, walking around the tree to make sure there were no more secret messages.

"So, he carved that into another tree?" Kyra asked.

"Yeah. I wonder if the old guy left it on trees all over the world."

"It's romantic," she said softly.

"It is now. When I first saw that, I remember curling my lip at the grossness of how anyone could like a girl."

She laughed. "Sounds like a ten-year-old boy who thinks girls are icky."

"But that was her lesson that day," he said, a little in

awe as the realization hit him. "That was the point she was trying to drive into my ten-year-old thick head. That girls aren't bad, but they are so...special."

"She probably worried that you wouldn't understand them with all those brothers."

"Exactly. So she took me to this tree and told me that someday, I would..." Damn it, his throat closed again.

"You would what, James?"

He would *love*. That's what she wanted for him—to love the way she and Dad did. He turned abruptly from the tree and let go of Kyra's hand, but she easily took his right back again.

"It must have broken your heart to lose her."

He closed his eyes, ready to leave, but she wasn't going to let him. "It broke everything," he admitted softly. "My heart, my family, and my spirit."

"Oh." She stroked his jaw with her thumbs as if her very touch could coax more words out of him. And it did. Words that needed to come out, whether he liked it or not. He wanted to look away, but Kyra's crystal-blue eyes held his gaze like magnets. He'd never told this to anyone, but right here, right now, with this woman under this tree, he had to.

"She went out for ice cream," he said. "We were playing a game of Monopoly, which, I can tell you, got crazy and competitive and cutthroat. And she decided we all needed ice cream in order to make the night perfect."

But the night had already been perfect, he thought. Nine Brannigans in the family room, a fire crackling, everyone just...content. *Nobody needed ice cream, damn it.*

"That night was..." How could he explain it to her? The before and after-ness of that moment in time. It was quite possibly the last time James had ever been fully and completely content. After that, nothing was ever the same. Nothing.

"Tell me, James," Kyra whispered.

"None of us wanted to leave the game." He cringed at the thought, feeling the pang of guilt that always tapped at his heart when he relived that evening. He *could* have gone with her. Should have. Maybe her life would have been spared if they'd just taken an extra minute getting out of the house. That's all. Ten seconds later, and there never would have been an accident.

"She insisted on running out alone, teasing us about how many gallons of ice cream it would take for all those boys." He could still see her vividly as she stood in the kitchen doorway, pointing at them. "'Be good or I'll bring back Rocky Road,' she said."

They all hated Rocky Road.

His whole body and soul drifted back to that night, the woodsy scent of the fire and the sound of little Finn's ringing laughter as they let him roll the dice. He could hear Hunter and Gabe whispering as they teamed up to beat everyone else, and remembered that Luke had nudged James's knee under the coffee table as if to say, *We could team up, too, and beat those two idiot twins.*

And Dad. Oh God, *Dad*.

Dad was sitting on the floor—when the hell had that ever happened since that night?—holding Finn on his lap and guiding Max and Knox, who were a little too young to be playing the game but refused to be left out.

Dad, who'd looked up at his wife with nothing but love and contentment in his eyes.

"'I'll hold down the fort, honey,'" James whispered out loud. "They were the last words my father ever spoke to his wife."

But he hadn't held down the fort. He'd disappeared into work and left the keys to the fort in James's hand, and thus began a lifetime of attempting to have control.

He closed his eyes, and something slipped in his heart, like a rock tumbling off a cliff. He could practically hear it fall and hit bottom and leave him...lighter.

Holy hell, he *had* let go of some of that grief.

Opening his eyes, he refocused on Kyra, seeing the tears in her eyes and one on her cheek. He wiped it away, then wrapped his arms around her and pulled her into his chest because...because he *had* to.

He had to cling to her, had to squeeze her hard, because...

Women leave.

The thought was random and rough, but so, so real in his heart. Women leave. And once they did, life was never the same.

Which would be why he'd never invited one to stay in his life. Except, why was he blaming all women for an accident that had taken his mother and changed his life? It wasn't her fault, and she didn't leave on purpose.

"What happened, James?" Kyra asked.

He swallowed, knowing he owed it to her to hear the whole story. "She was less than a mile from our ranch when a young driver, a kid who'd gotten his license the day before, whipped around a blind corner and plowed into her."

Kyra gasped. "Oh God." Then she pressed her hand on his face again. "No wonder you hate turns like that. I understand now."

Was that the reason? He'd never put those two things together, but it made sense. *Kyra* made sense. So much sense. He held her close, squeezing her a little.

"She was in a coma for about a week, then she died,"

he finished. "And that was the end of the perfect Brannigan family."

"With all that love and stability?" She sounded stunned. "I have no doubt her death left a hole in your life, but seven kids and a loving father—"

"He died a little with her," James said. "He was never quite the same, and honestly, she was truly the glue that held it all together. Her infectious joy. Her crazy ideas and spontaneous acts of...fun."

She gave him a wry smile. "And now we know why you hate fun."

He pulled her all the way into him, pressing a kiss on her sweet-smelling hair.

"I don't hate it." He tipped her face up. "In fact, it's growing on me. And so are you, lemondrop. You and your brand of magic, which makes me talk and laugh and do crazy things...like this." He pressed his lips on hers, lightly at first, easy and gentle.

"Mmm. Not crazy," she murmured into his mouth. "Delicious."

He intensified the kiss, backing her into the thick tree trunk so he could feel her pressed against him. She wrapped her arms around his neck and kissed him with all the passion that bubbled in her, purring each time his hands coasted up and down her sides and lingered at her breasts.

"James," she whispered.

"Mmmm." He kissed down her jaw to her throat.

"I feel like your parents are watching."

He froze, and couldn't help laughing. "You do?"

"Well, this is their place. For all we know, they made love here."

His eyes widened in horror. "Why did you say that?"

"Did it kill the mood?"

"A little." He held her waist and eased her against him. "You know something?"

"What?"

He put both hands on her face and inched her closer. "I want to make love to you and not under a tree."

Her lips curved up. "You do?"

"Come back to the hotel with me," he whispered. "And don't leave. Don't leave for days and nights and days and nights. How's that for fun?" It might not seem like it was to her, but to him, it was a monumental change and loss of control and step forward.

And he wanted to take it. With Kyra.

"So. Much. Fun." She let her eyes shutter close and answered with another kiss, this one a deep, soulful promise of paradise.

Chapter Fourteen

Kyra careened down the mountain on the motor scooter, doing her best not to risk their lives but giving the bike plenty of speed to get them to where they both wanted to be.

In bed together.

She was breathless by the time they parked the bike outside of the Eden Roc, shaking as James whisked her through the lobby so none of the friendly staff could stop them, and helpless when he pressed her against the elevator wall before the doors fully closed.

Alone, he kissed her while they rode, holding her body, touching and caressing, anxious to finally enjoy every inch.

Upstairs, they broke the kiss, blinking, neither one focused or balanced. Half laughing, half sighing, he led her to the suite, nudged her inside, shut and locked the door as he pinned her with a hungry gaze.

"Kyra," he whispered, his breath as strangled as hers. "Finally."

"Finally?" She laughed softly. "I've known you less than a week, James."

Holding her face in his hands, he kissed her again, more tenderly this time, taking a moment to explore her lower lip and let their tongues get even better acquainted. "But I wanted you from the minute you blasted me with your first ray of sunshine."

He threaded his fingers into her hair and kissed some more, guiding her deeper into the suite, heading for the bedroom.

"You thought I was ditzy," she said between kisses.

"No, just...perky." He started working on the buttons of her sleeveless top. "And you thought I was an asshole."

She helped with the last button and shrugged it off as they reached the bedroom door. "No, just...jerky."

He barked a laugh at her rhyme. "Honestly, Kyra. I wanted you since the moment you breezed in front of me and started...melting me with warmth."

She dragged her hand down his chest over his shirt, her destination clear. When she got there, she put her hand over the huge bulge in his pants. "Nothing has *melted*."

"Except..." He closed his eyes, clearly stopping himself from finishing.

"Except what?" she asked.

He shook his head, reaching around her back to get to her bra clasp. "Your clothes. They are about to melt off. And then your body is going to melt in my mouth."

"Promises, promises."

He slid her bra straps down her shoulders, his gaze smoldering as he stared at her bare breasts. "Just like I thought."

"What? Perky?"

"Pretty."

"Pretty what?" she teased.

"Pretty perfect, like the rest of you."

He kissed down her throat and covered one breast with a sure, warm touch and sucked the other one.

Somehow, she got him to stop long enough to tug his shirt over his head.

She sighed noisily at the sight of his bare chest. She'd seen it before—she'd admired the hell out of it before—but this was different. Now his body was hers to explore and taste and adore.

At the bed, he eased her down on her back and hovered over her, suddenly still for a moment as he searched her face.

"Second thoughts?" she asked, a twinge of fear twisting her chest.

"Are you kidding?" He stroked her cheek, catching his breath, lost in his thoughts.

"What is it?" she asked.

"I've never known anyone quite like you."

"We've established I'm not your type, James."

"I don't even know what that means," he said. "But if I had a type, she'd be warm and funny and sexy and bright and beautiful, and God, I sound like an idiot, but I have to tell you this."

He didn't sound like an idiot. He sounded like a lover, and it was so sweet that she swallowed against a thick throat, as hungry for his compliments and feelings as she was for his body.

"I'm just trying to say that I don't take you for granted. Now hang on and don't you move."

It surprised her when he got off the bed, but he only went into the bathroom and came back with a foil packet, tossing the condom on the bed next to her. "Where were we?"

"Right where we're supposed to be." She pulled him down, exploring abs that were taut and delicious, with a sexy trail that led down to the button and zipper her hands itched to open.

The first pull of an orgasm tortured her already, making her skin tight and tingly, and her hips moved against him like she had no control. He worked his mouth and hands down her belly, and all she could do was tunnel her fingers into his thick hair, holding his head as he kissed her, sighing as he tugged off the white jeans she'd thought would be perfect for a day of sightseeing.

She studied the angle of his broad shoulders, the olive tone of his skin, and the way his hair feathered over his neck.

She was sightseeing all right. Beautiful, sexy sights.

At her appreciative moan, he looked up at her, a smile in his dark eyes. "Even your panties are yellow." He dipped a teasing finger into the silky thong. "Definitely your color, sunshine."

Had she made that decision subconsciously this morning?

"Sunny. I was going for *sexy* right now."

"Trust me, you are that."

She sucked in a breath as he circled her most tender spot, already aching with need and ready for him. Whispering his name, she spread her legs as he slowly, easily, crazily eased one finger into her.

Biting her lip so she didn't cry out, she moved with him as he found a rhythm that matched the slamming beat of her heart. He brought her right to the painful precipice of an orgasm and then worked his way back up to kiss her some more.

He slid his tongue in and out of her mouth like a foreshadowing of what his body was about to do to her. She sucked his tongue, bit his lip and, with trembling hands, unzipped his shorts. Finally, she closed her hand over a mighty, thick erection.

He moaned as she stroked him, then reached for the condom and tore the packet with his teeth, enough desperation in the move to take her a little closer to the same edge. He held her gaze as he sheathed himself, the only sound in the room their ragged, uneven breaths. She searched his face, memorizing every feature and line, the slackness of his jaw as he fought for air, the darkness of his eyes as he studied her right back.

She grazed his cheek, touched again by his words and by his restraint at a moment when most men wouldn't exhibit any at all. "You're special, too." At his look, she stilled her fingers. "Especially when you let your walls down."

His eyes closed partway. "I don't know how you do that…"

She smiled, dragging her hand from his face, over his chest, and down to his hard-on, guiding him to her. "Like this, James. We do that just…like…this."

He kissed her hungrily as he found his way inside her, very slowly and easily at first, building to a perfect tempo and speed with each increasingly deep thrust.

He filled her, hot, hard, and thick, plunging in and out and never, not once, breaking the kiss. His mouth was as sexy as his body, as intense and warm and wet. His weight was secure and masculine, his legs strong as she wrapped her thighs around his to get every inch of him inside her.

He murmured her name, groaning with raw, ragged pleasure, both of them lost as an incendiary heat built. She fell first, giving in to the ribbon of desire that wrapped through her body, squeezing a climax out of her, blinding her with bliss.

After she came, he surrendered to the same power, moving ferociously in and out of her, his breath like growls, his hands grasping her until he lost all shred of control and spilled into her over and over again.

Finally, his full weight pressed on her, his mouth against her ear, every breath an effort.

"Lemondrop," he managed to whisper.

She wanted to smile at the ridiculous nickname, but it took too much work to move a single muscle.

"I'm in trouble."

"Why?" she managed to ask.

"Because I'm still inside you, and I already want more."

"Mmmm. Why is that a problem? I'll stay all night."

He let out a sigh. "No one ever stays."

She lifted her hands and put them on his face, forcing his head up so he had to look at her. "Didn't you just tell me I'm not like anyone else?"

"Yeah." He searched her eyes, something that looked an awful lot like fear in his. "That's why I'm in trouble."

She thought he was kidding. Of course she did. Sunny, bright, warm, completely adorable, and totally honest Kyra Summers didn't know that icy, cold, heartless James Brannigan had arrived in Italy with one plan: to sell the winery she and her adopted family loved so much.

And that's why he was in trouble.

Still grappling with the decision, he left her sleeping in his bed, naked and spent. As hard as it was to walk away—and damn, it was, because she was so silky and warm and womanly and perfect—he got up, pulled on some shorts, and went out to the balcony, his gaze drawn to a sunset faded by a thick band of silvery clouds that hovered over the mountain and warned of an early evening shower.

JAMES

Deep in his gut, the weather mirrored his mood. Churned up. Confused. Hazy where there should be nothing but sunshine.

Why would he feel that way? He just had sex with a hot and willing woman, and he should be satisfied, content, and replete with a sense that everything was just fine.

But something wasn't fine, and he knew it. Was this just garden-variety fear of a commitment? Resentment that someone got behind his walls? Or was it something deeper?

He didn't get crippled by emotions and attachments, because he didn't have time or interest in such things. He made a point of being sure that even a "girlfriend"—and there'd been mighty few of those—knew he preferred to wake up alone.

Why was that?

He had no idea. Just that the women in his life had accepted that, along with all the perks that came with dating a wealthy, attentive man.

He felt his lip curl in an unexpected bout of self-disgust. Was he that much of a coldhearted bastard? Was his coldness purely self-preservation because there were so many women who wanted his name, his bank account, and his access to society? Or was that an instinctive act to protect his heart because…

Women leave.

Okay, one fairly important woman in his life left, but not by choice. She died. And when she did, James started putting that wall around him brick by brick. If this woman took those walls down, then what? Would he feel raw all the time? Vulnerable? Out of control? Wretched when someone who bounced around the world like a rubber ball left him? Because she would. He knew she—

"Pretty lonely out here, isn't it?"

He turned at the sound of Kyra's voice, inhaling softly at the sight that accompanied it. She'd wrapped the sheet around her, holding it in a bunch just above her breasts. Her hair was tousled, wild, like a waterfall of blond silk tumbling over her bare shoulders. Her eyes were sleepy and her lips a tiny bit swollen from all the kissing.

Good God, she was stunning.

"I needed..." Air. Time. *You. So much more of you.*

"Space," she supplied when he couldn't finish the sentence.

"No." He took a step forward, reaching to draw her closer to him, aching already to touch her.

"Then why did you leave me?"

Because I know you'll leave me.

The realization gutted him for a moment. "I had some things to work out." Like the fact that he had been planning to sell the winery. It would be so easy to tell her now, but he couldn't bear to see the hurt and shock and disappointment on her face. Not when she looked so beautiful and well-loved.

When she found out, would she leave?

Better to tell her later, when it was an idea he'd killed, not a plan he had.

"Just for the record, James Brannigan, you're not my type, either."

He thumbed her cheek, aware of the mist hovering over the two of them as the rainstorm got closer. "I bet I'm not," he agreed. "For one thing, I don't do fun."

She smiled at him. "What we just spent the last hour doing? *Epic* fun."

"You probably like a guy who's passionate and colorful. Someone who'll jump on a motor scooter, pick olives, and...and...kiss in the rain."

"Rain's coming, big guy. Now's your chance." A breeze lifted a strand of her hair, the air cooling, either from the pending storm or the slight hitch they'd just hit in their fledgling romance. "But that's not what I meant about my type. I meant what you are, who you are, what you…represent."

He frowned, trying to figure out what he *represented* to her. "I could go so many ways here. A foreigner? An investor? A chickenshit scooter rider?"

She laughed. "I can teach you not to be scared of that," she said, but her laugh faded. "But I can't teach you how to…" She put one hand on his bare chest. "How to use this incredible heart of yours."

"What does that mean, exactly?"

She slowly dropped her hand and turned to the vista, sighing. "When I was a little girl," she finally said, "I used to have my nannies buy me every shade made of colored Post-it Notes."

He lifted his brows, the statement so out of left field, he wasn't sure where she could be going with this.

"My first introduction to them was through my mother," she said. "They would be stuck all over the many piles of paper she had from work, like brightly colored flower petals, pink and neon green, yellow and baby blue. They meant something to her, I realized at a young age. I would lie in bed next to her in the evenings while she was on the phone with her bosses reporting in from a day's work, and she would write words on those little papers and stick them somewhere to be noticed and remembered."

Her voice hitched a little, and she blinked, as if caught off guard by the emotion this revelation caused.

"So I used to ask my nannies to buy Post-it Notes for me, in the wildest possible colors they could find. And then…" She looked at him, a little embarrassment in her expression. "I would leave a pack of them next to my mother's bed with a pen because I wanted her to write me a note before she went to work. So I would have it all day."

"Did she?"

"Once or twice. When I'd have a nanny who knew what was what and reminded her. Once I tried leaving her a note, a pale pink Post-it shaped like a heart that Miss Susan found…" Her smile grew wistful and her gaze moved from him back to the view, but focused on another place and time. "I put it on a document that she needed, and I must have covered something important." She shook her head. "She was not thrilled with me for that."

He stroked her bare shoulder.

"I stopped waiting for those notes after a while," she whispered. "And when I finished high school, a few days after I turned eighteen, I left home and started traveling the world."

He considered that, scanning her face, taking in the weird way their histories were similar, but different. "She sacrificed a lot for work."

She gave a mirthless laugh. "Precisely. She sacrificed me. And I will never give my heart to someone who puts work and money before me." She leaned into him. "My body? Yes, I obviously am willing to do that. But nothing else."

He got the subtext of what she was saying, not that there was anything too subtle about it. He was a workaholic, he was coldhearted, and she'd slept with him but would never feel anything. And if she found out he'd done it while considering an opportunity to sell the winery?

JAMES

He didn't even want to think about how much that would hurt her.

After a moment, she glanced at him again. "So we have that in common with our mothers."

"I doubt mine ever saw a Post-it Note," James said. "But if she did, it was to remind her of football practice."

"I meant our mothers screwed us both up."

He frowned at her, not following. "I must have given you the wrong impression, then. She never screwed me up."

Had she? He looked away, back to the foggy clouds building and bringing rain, but he didn't see this new take on the postcard view. He just saw…Kathleen Brannigan. Turning, rushing, flipping her hand to wave good-bye.

That moment when the Brannigan family cracked in half, at least in his opinion. The moment when he learned that if he didn't control everything…everything could disappear.

So maybe she did screw him up a little.

"James," she whispered, sidling closer to him. "Here comes the rain."

As if on cue, the first drop hit his bare shoulder. And her face. And his head. "And you want to stand out here and kiss in the rain."

She threw a glance at the chaise lounge. "Why stop with kissing?"

The wind picked up as the rain fell in earnest, wetting her hair and sending an unexpected chill over both of them. He tangled his fingers in her pale gold locks, as lost in her hair as he was in her eyes. "You want to stay out here and get soaking wet for the sheer fun of it."

She loosened her grip on the sheet. "No one can see us."

His body stirred at the thought, but his brain immediately took over. He reached for the material she held, taking it from her fingers to knot the fabric securely around her. "There," he said. "I've got it."

"You like things safe, don't you?"

He considered that, then nodded. "You take care of six hooligans under the age of ten when no parents are around. You'd get cautious, too."

She angled her head toward the chaise. "Come on, Brannigan. Sex in the rain will cure what ails you."

"Sex…in the rain."

With a slow, sweet, sly smile, she flicked the knot he'd just made and let the wet material fall to the balcony floor. Naked, she looked up at him with a dare in her eyes, as if to say…lose control. *Lose it, James.*

And he did.

He pulled her naked body into him and kissed her hard on the mouth, closing his eyes, not caring that the rain drenched them.

Not caring about anything, really.

"*You* cure what ails me," he murmured as he pulled them both down on the chaise.

She just let out one of her musical laughs and climbed on top of him while the rain fell and washed away everything but Kyra.

Chapter Fifteen

Kyra drifted out of a deep sleep, a slow, easy, lazy awakening that gave her a chance to appreciate every sensation her body was experiencing. Cool, expensive cotton sheets grazed her arms and legs. A heavy, possessive arm rested around her waist, nestling her back into warm skin and hard muscles. Masculine, sleep-heavy breaths ruffled the back of her hair and told her James was still asleep. Opening one eye to gauge the light between the closed shutters, she guessed it was not yet five in the morning.

The sun would be up around six, which was when she normally rose, took coffee outside on the veranda, and watched the day unfold with golden rays over acres of grape vines, lemon trees, and olive groves. But today? All she wanted to do was stay in this bed, in these arms, with this man.

She probably should have slipped away in the middle of the night, just to avoid the questions Anamaria would ask when she found Kyra's bed untouched. No judgment, just questions. Kyra was thirty years old, and no one at the winery expected her to live like a nun, despite the fact that she'd done exactly that since she'd arrived in Positano.

But James Brannigan was their boss. The owner. The caller of the shots and the keeper of their future. She was taking a huge risk sleeping with him.

She didn't care. She'd take any risk necessary for another night like this past one. Her body was sore and spent, touched and kissed and caressed in places that she'd practically forgotten about. She ached from hours of making love and tingled from the need to do it all over again.

He'd already broken his personal "no overnight" rule with her. Surely he had a limit on how many times he could be with a woman before it became too much like a commitment. And no doubt he put strict parameters on what could be said outside the bedroom and how close and honest and intimate they could be.

She smiled sleepily. Well, they'd been awfully close and honest and intimate last night. Her stomach did a little flip just thinking about how beautiful it was to watch James's walls tumble down.

With each confession and kiss, his expression softened. With each memory and secret they shared, his laugh grew easier and more frequent. With each exchange of pleasure they gave to each other, his icy exterior melted into affectionate and…loving.

Could that last, or was it merely the aftereffects of ridiculously good sex?

Her eyes popped open at the sound of a loud hum and a ding from somewhere on the floor.

James groaned.

"That's your phone, I think," Kyra said, knowing hers didn't make any sounds like that.

"What time is it?" he mumbled, instinctively pulling her closer and sliding his hand up to possessively cover her breast.

JAMES

"Five-ish."

"Mmm. Eleven at night in New York. Can't be important." He rubbed his thumb over her nipple, which was sore and tender from all the attention, but beaded under his fingertip anyway. "Not as important as this."

Against her backside, she felt his erection grow, closing her eyes and sighing as he started moving against her, the rhythm already natural. After one night. How did that happen?

The phone quieted, and they contentedly lay in the dark, in a sweet, comfortable silence.

And the phone hummed and dinged again.

"Damn it," he muttered, pushing away to roll out of bed and poke around on the floor. Kyra turned, her eyes adjusted enough to appreciate his naked body as he bent over to seize the phone and fell back into bed with her, squinting at it.

"FaceTime?" he said, scowling at the device. "Freaking Luke is FaceTiming me?"

"Your brother?" she asked, snuggling closer. "Does he normally do that?"

"No. None of us does. Email and text are our preferred forms of communication unless it's..." His voice trailed off, and she nudged him.

"Take the call, James. It could be important. I'll stay over here out of camera range."

He snorted and pulled her closer, then threw a look at her. "Or would you prefer that?"

She nodded and slid away to the other side of the bed as he tapped the phone.

"James! Bro, good morning!"

"How's Italy, big guy?"

"Did we wake you?"

It was more than one brother, that was for sure. Kyra

scooted a little closer to get a peek at the small phone screen.

"What the hell is up with you two?" James asked, rubbing sleep from his eyes. "If you know I'm in Italy, you know it's five in the morning."

"Eight at night here in Yosemite."

"Knox? Is that you?" James peered at the phone. "Oh, that's right. Gabe told me you and...*Erin*"—he said the name with extra emphasis, as if to prove he remembered it—"are staying at Algoma in Yosemite with Luke."

"We are," he answered. "The girls all went out horseback riding today, and then they wanted a night out for dinner. So Luke and I, uh, might have put back a few shots of Bushmills 21. It *was* Dad's favorite whiskey."

"So you thought you'd drunk-dial me." He rolled his eyes and threw a glance at Kyra, who bit back a laugh, slipping closer to see the faces and somehow know more about this mysterious band of Brannigan brothers.

"How can I thank you, Knox?" James asked wryly.

So that was Knox. Kyra squinted to get a better look, instantly seeing the family resemblance with dark hair and dark eyes. Knox's hair was much longer, though, nearly grazing his muscular shoulders, and his whole demeanor was utterly chill. Although that could have been the Bushmills 21.

"So, how's that bike running?" James asked.

Ah, yes. Knox was the one who inherited a vintage motorcycle when their dad died. Last night, during one of their long conversations, James had told her stories about each of his brothers, detailing their "legacies" from Colin Brannigan and sharing their distinct personalities.

"It cruises nicely around Cinnabar," he said,

JAMES

reminding Kyra that Knox was the brother who loved nothing more than a good time. "You know I'm living there with Erin now."

"Yeah, I know," James said. "No more secret businesses you haven't told us about owning?"

Knox laughed, that same easy laugh she heard from James in his looser moments. "Dude, I've found my calling. I still have a lot of investments—no hedge funds like yours, but the restaurant, a surf shop, and that trendy shoelace company. Don't judge."

"Judge? I never mock a smart investment, my friend. What about that card game? I'm still ready to drop some dollars into it."

Knox smiled at that, a sly smile that took any edge out of his handsome face and made him seem far more approachable than James when she'd first met him.

"I'll hit you up when I need you," Knox said. "Fact is, I'm the one getting proposals for small businesses, and I happen to love investing in them. Erin really helped me realize that."

"My little brother the capitalist." James sounded truly proud. "Couldn't be happier. What's Luke up to?"

The phone got handed to the other man, giving Kyra a chance to surreptitiously meet yet another Brannigan, even if it was in 2-D. Jeez, were they all hot as hell?

Luke had the same dark hair and dark eyes, but even without the scruffy cheeks that Knox had, he somehow looked more rugged and outdoorsy than either James or Knox. Not a man who cared about investments at all, but…what had James told her last night?

Adventure was his drug of choice and what drove Luke to create life-risking documentaries. Right this moment, he didn't look like he was risking anything but another shot of whiskey.

"We've been talking about you, man," he said, his expression far more serious than Knox's. "We know why you're in Italy and called because…" Luke glanced next to him and reached the phone out farther, so the screen showed both men.

"You're dealing with your legacy," Knox finished.

Instantly, James sat up, going from sweetly sleepy to fully alert. "Yep. Dealing with it right now."

"How?" Luke demanded.

"Just checking it out." He was out of bed in a second, swooping up boxers from the floor, his body tense as his gaze moved to his desk and his jaw tightened. "Figuring out what to do."

A chill tingled her skin. *Figuring out what to do?*

What did that mean?

She couldn't see the screen but heard Knox say, "You gotta listen to us, dude. Luke and I have had a revelation." He dragged the word out, making Luke laugh as if they'd shared an inside joke. Or were drunk.

James was already in the hall. "Listen, maybe you two ought to call someone who might be drinking as much as you, cause this is not a good time to discuss this." His voice was cold and humorless, the way he was on business calls.

Even to his family?

Their voices and response drifted off as James walked down the hall into the living room. In a second, she heard the balcony doors open and close, silencing Kyra's ability to hear any more of the conversation.

She pulled the fluffy comforter higher over her naked body, a sense of foreboding pressing on her. What did he mean by *figuring out what to do* with the winery? Why wouldn't he talk to her about it?

And why had he stared at his desk with a little bit

JAMES

of…terror? That's what it was. That same look she saw in the rearview mirror on the motor scooter. What was on that desk?

Kyra slipped out of bed with none of the purpose that had just driven James away. No, she moved in raw fear, not surprised that she trembled a little as she stood and looked at the papers piled up on the wooden surface that ran almost the width of the room under a row of windows.

She eyed his closed laptop. A soft-sided leather briefcase. Documents…*with Post-it Notes*.

Her heart dropped. How much like her mother, the cold and calculating closer, was he?

Didn't she have a right to know about the man who held the future of the winery in his hands? About the man who held *her* in his hands?

She tiptoed to that desk and visually skimmed the papers. There was just enough visible to read without actually touching anything that didn't belong to her. Spreadsheets and memos, letters and contracts. It all reminded her so much of her mother.

And there, partially under a stack of other papers, was some letterhead that said Whitehouse Wineries.

She knew who they were, of course. Anyone remotely connected to the winemaking industry knew Whitehouse. A company known to be huge, faceless, driven by the bottom line, and known for swallowing up…

"Oh God." She put her hand over her mouth as the reality of this hit her. She had to know. Had to. Reaching a trembling hand, she lifted the papers that covered the page with the letterhead and squinted, leaning closer to read just the first few words, knowing that what she was doing was so very wrong.

It was a memo.

To: James Brannigan

From: William Hayward

Subj: Sale of Villa Pietro to Whitehouse Status Report

She literally reeled at the words. He was selling the winery. Her gaze shifted to the date—five days ago.

Every single minute he'd been here, he'd had this plan.

Every minute of the last twelve hours. They'd made love, talked, laughed, had dinner brought up and ate it in robes on the balcony after the rain ended, made love again, slept, cuddled, whispered, and she'd been ready to let him inside her again.

And all along he was planning to sell.

She stared at the words and tried to breathe, but couldn't.

Chapter Sixteen

James stood on the balcony where hours before he'd lost himself with the sweetest, brightest, most delightful lover he'd ever known.

He glanced over his shoulder into the suite as Luke droned on about the film he was making about climbing El Capitan, which was near the resort that had been his legacy.

While Luke talked, James replayed earlier snippets of the conversation. How much of that had she heard? Enough. Anyway, there was no hiding it from her now. He had to tell her, as soon as he got these drunken clowns off the phone.

"So I'm not completely housebroken," Luke said on a laugh. "'Cause I have a feeling you think Knox and I are totally whipped by these women we love."

Did he think that? "If whipped sounds content and stable," he said. "Because you both seem to be."

"Dude, you have no idea." Knox grabbed the phone again, his eyes bright from the Bushmills. Or love. Who could tell the difference? Both had made him loopy. "Erin changed me. And Luke says the same thing about Lizzie. Don't you see?"

He peered out to the predawn darkness of the

Mediterranean. "See what?" he asked, too tired and anxious to get back to Kyra to have a philosophical discussion with his whiskey-soaked brothers.

"It was Dad's doing," Luke said. "I mean, in my case, it was conscious. He knew Lizzie was at the resort."

"So he set you up by leaving the place to you?" James asked.

"Yeah, but it's more than that," Luke said. "Being here helped me get to know a part of the old man that I honestly never appreciated before. He loved his family."

La famiglia è tutto. James choked. "Yeah, I knew that."

"It was different for you," Knox added. "You remember him before Mom died. We don't. I was a little kid, and the only dad I knew was the one who was basically ashamed of me because I didn't take life seriously enough."

James nodded, settling on the chaise and holding the phone so he could really see his brothers while they talked. Telling Kyra the truth was important, but this was, too. His brothers deserved his attention, whether they were drunk or sober.

"It made me mad," Knox said. "And resentful. But then I found out that he had my back all along. And knowing Erin—who I'd have never met if Dad hadn't left me that motorcycle—really helped me see him differently. And, by extension, myself."

James took a deep, slow breath, and Luke laughed. "I think our big brother just rolled his eyes."

"No, I didn't," he said. "It's early, this is deep, but I…"

"Don't really want to think about it," Luke supplied.

"But I have to." James ran his free hand through his

hair. "I'm also grappling with why the hell I have this winery. Dad could have sold it and made just as much money. It wasn't difficult to get an offer, but now..."

"He sent you there for a reason," Knox said.

James looked over his shoulder into the living room, catching a glimpse of movement. It was Kyra, fully dressed and putting her shoes on near the door. Oh *shit*.

"I gotta go," he said quickly, standing up.

"James, listen to me," Luke pleaded. "Don't miss the big picture. Don't miss what's really important. Don't miss Dad's last lesson."

Screw lessons. She was leaving. "Okay, got it. I have to go. She's..." She was digging her keys out of her bag. He threw open the French door.

"*She?*" Both brothers repeated the word, loudly and with much amusement and emphasis, making Kyra whip around from the door to the suite.

"Holy shit, bro," Knox said on a laugh. "You, too?"

"No," James insisted. "It's just...nothing."

As soon as he said it, he saw the flash of hurt in her eyes. Son of a bitch! "I have to go. Thanks for the drunk-dial." Without waiting for their good-byes, he thumbed the phone and threw it on the living room sofa, walking toward her.

"Are you leaving?"

"You're planning to sell the winery." She threw the statement down like a gauntlet, with nothing but challenge in her gaze. No, there was something more than a challenge there. Pain. Shadows of deep, soul-slicing pain.

"Damn it, I knew you'd misconstrue what you heard them say—"

"Misconstrue?" She paled. "And now you're going to lie to me."

"I'm not…" He exhaled, a long slow sigh of resignation. Yeah, damn it. He was lying to her. "I *was* going to sell it." Which made him scum in her eyes. In anyone's eyes. "But I changed my mind," he added quickly.

"Really? When?" she fired back. "Because the memo about the status on the sale to Whitehouse Wineries would say differently."

Shit. He tried for the offense. "You looked through my stuff?"

"The stuff that was on the desk in the room where I just trusted you completely for twelve solid hours?"

The offense failed.

He took a few steps closer, his penetrating gaze searching her face, looking for the sunshine he'd come to adore but seeing only ice in her eyes. "I didn't want to hurt you or make you mad or any of those things."

"Too late." She crossed her arms protectively. "I'm *all* of those things."

"Kyra." He reached for her hand, but she snapped away before he could touch her. "Yes, I came here with that intention, but after yesterday…"

"Sex changed your mind?" She snorted. "Great. The 'get cozy' plan really worked. The family will be so proud."

Her sarcasm sliced him. She was never bitter, never dark, but he'd made her that way. "Not sex. What Anamaria told me. And then at the tree. Everything. I realized it was the wrong thing to do."

"No, James. Not telling me was the wrong thing to do."

No kidding. "I was just talking to my brothers about it—"

"I thought you were talking to them about *nothing*."

JAMES

She threw the word at him. "Like how to make the most amount of money on the sale of a little winery that means *nothing* to you but everything to me? Or was it how the woman you spent the night with is, what was the word, *nothing?* Oh, yeah. Nothing. Just a little lemondrop of *nothing.*"

She turned and snagged her purse from the table, and he was next to her in a second.

"Stop it!" He got a hold of her shoulders before she could get away. "If you'd heard the whole conversation, you'd know my brothers are on your side."

"We have sides now? Who knew? Oh, you did. You just forgot to mention it to me." Her eyes shuttered closed as she tried to wrest from his grasp, but he held tight.

"Listen to me. Of course I intended to sell it originally, that's what I do—"

She got free and glared at him. "Do you know how many times I heard my mother justify her wretched job with those words? And this isn't just any company you're heartlessly dismantling. This is *my* family now."

"I'm not heartlessly dismantling anything, Kyra."

"No, but Whitehouse Wineries will."

He couldn't even argue with that. "Kyra, before I did anything at all, I wanted to know if I could figure out what my dad had in mind. Because Luke and Knox and even Gabe seem to think I'm supposed to…" He fisted his hands. "I'm supposed to…"

"To what?"

Good God, could he even say it? He stared into her eyes, took a breath, and jumped. "Change."

"What does that mean?"

"I don't know," he admitted. "But I don't want to hide the truth from you any longer. I did plan to sell the winery. I did. But I can change that decision, and I will."

She looked at him for a long time, her expression confused and broken and nothing like the satisfied, loving woman he'd fallen asleep with.

He'd wrecked this.

"I don't believe you," she said simply. "I need to talk to the family. *My* family. Because that's what those people are, James. They are the family I never had, and I can assure you, I will pick them over anyone in the world, including you."

She stepped back and turned to the door, her bag on her shoulder, her keys in her hand.

"Kyra." He heard the crack in his voice but didn't care. "Please don't leave."

"I have to," she said. "Good-bye."

Without waiting for a response, she slipped out the door, proving once again that women leave.

And that wasn't what he wanted. Not this time. Not this woman.

"I know what he's going to do."

Every eye around the kitchen table turned to Kyra as she stood in the doorway of the kitchen. The response was fast, furious, and, oh God, loud.

"Where you been?"

"All night, *Cara*?"

"We almost send the *polizia* after you."

"You call this *cozy*?"

Kyra held up her hand for mercy. "I haven't had coffee yet. And I need it, fam. I need it." But she loved them for wondering and worrying more about her than the future of the winery. That would change soon enough.

The questions stopped while she took her seat at the table and accepted a steaming cup from Anamaria, avoiding direct eye contact with the old woman's judgmental gaze.

Instead, Kyra stared at the table and took a long drink. Then another.

"Why you no talk?" Anamaria demanded.

"Because none of you are going to be happy with what I have to say," she whispered, finally looking up, but just seeing a sea of faces that she thought of as family. None of them looked remotely like her, that was for sure, but all of them mattered. So, so much.

Her gaze shifted to Lorenzo and Elena, who sat side by side, holding hands, staring at her, fear mixed with worry and no small amount of fury, all directed at her. Because they loved her.

Next to them, Enzo and Filippa each held the hand of one of their sons, who were unnaturally quiet, as if even little Nico and Gianni knew something was about to rock their perfect little worlds.

Across the table, Antonio held a biscuit poised in midair, unable to bite as he waited, and Sofia rubbed her enormous belly. Would their baby girl not get to grow up in this happy, solid home?

"Tell us, Kyra," Bruno demanded, his voice as dark as his eyes on her. "Tell us what you learned from all this time with *Signor* Brannigan."

One more sip of coffee. One more look around the table. One more moment of utopia in Italy before it all falls apart.

"He's selling to Whitehouse Wineries," she said softly, although she might as well have thrown a bomb on the table and let it explode. Questions, exclamations, and demands followed, along with so many gesturing hands that she could have sworn she felt a breeze.

Lorenzo won the battle of the wills, silencing them all when he slammed the table and shouted a few choice Italian curses. Every mouth stopped moving, and the only sound was the clicking of alabaster beads as Anamaria slid her rosary out of her pocket.

"Are you certain?" Elena asked Kyra.

Was she? To be fair, James said he wouldn't sell. But why hadn't he told her he had an offer in the first place? So he could sleep with her? The thought stabbed. "Not certain, but the offer is on the table, and he is talking to them." That much she *was* certain of.

"Then you must get it off the table!" Anamaria said. "Get more cozy!"

She managed a smile. "Nonna, I got about as cozy as I can get. If he changes his mind, it won't be my doing. I'm..." She closed her eyes briefly. "Too emotionally invested."

Most of them looked like they didn't understand the term, and she was too drained to try to explain. Anyway, she'd been gone overnight. They knew where she'd been and no doubt knew exactly what she'd been doing.

Bruno stood suddenly, his mouth turned down. "I need to leave," he announced in Italian.

Kyra sighed and looked up at him, searching his face. Bruno was like a brother to her—and that's all he'd ever been. They both knew it, and they both preferred it that way. Didn't they? Something was making him frown and drag his hands through his hair.

"Where are you going?" Lorenzo demanded.

"Wine shipment goes out later this week. Did you forget?" Bruno asked. "Antonio needs to get in the cellar, and you need to supervise the help, and I'm going to meet with the truckers who are in Naples now waiting for me. I don't want them to hear this from someone who knows this...this *Whitehouse*."

He'd spoken quickly, and in Italian, but Kyra got it all. Bruno, for all his immaturity, bravado, and carousing, was wise enough to know they couldn't let this news bring the business of the winery to a halt.

But no one else moved, all of them looking at Lorenzo, waiting for his order.

He whispered something under his breath and turned to his wife. "Do you have all of the papers ready?"

She nodded. "Enzo and I finished them early this morning. We can give them to him now."

Lorenzo turned to Antonio. "You are ready for this shipment?"

He lifted a broad shoulder as if to ask how his father could question that.

Finally, Lorenzo looked at his mother. "Have you said every prayer?"

She lifted the rosary. "I called up to Giorgio last night," she said. "He say what he always say. *La famiglia è tutto*."

Of course. The family is everything.

At Anamaria's words, they all nodded solemnly, the abrupt explosion of emotion soothed already.

"*Tutto*," Lorenzo said softly. Then he looked at Kyra, uncharacteristically silent for a moment. "We will survive," he said. "We will be strong and do what is required and continue to make the best wine in the region, the country, even the world."

"But..." Kyra shook her head, not following. "If this big corporate winery comes in and replaces all of you, then what?"

Lorenzo crossed his arms, smug and arrogant and certain. "We will still be *famiglia*. We will find work, a winery, food, and shelter. We will survive as one," he said, his tone indicating his disappointment, or even frustration, that she didn't understand that.

She didn't. "How?" she asked.

"As a *family*," he said, speaking the word slowly in English, as if she was the one who didn't understand the language. Well, she didn't understand this *attitude*, that was for sure. Didn't they realize how tenuous this situation was?

Bruno put his cup on the counter and pointed to his father. "*Sì, sì.* I go now."

Antonio pushed up. "I will be in the cellars."

Elena grabbed some papers. "We'll finish this work," she said, nudging Enzo to join her in the office.

"Nico, Gianni." Filippa pulled back their bench. "*Venite, venite.* It is time for school," she said. "English today. I teach you." She smiled at Kyra. "Because you teach me."

Suddenly, the table was empty as the family moved off to their respective jobs in the winery and places in life. The blow had been dealt, and they would endure it and move on.

They would. As a family. The one she didn't actually belong to.

Alone at the table, Kyra looked down at her coffee as the sounds of Sebastianis hustling around faded. She wasn't part of this *famiglia*, just like those painful summers when she went to her father's home in Georgia and sat at their table as an outsider.

She wanted to belong, but wanting didn't make it so.

Here, she was an outsider, a guest, an employee. She didn't know how the Sebastianis would survive, but they would. And she would simply…move on.

"*Cara.*"

Kyra startled at the pressure of Anamaria's hand on her shoulder. She looked up and realized her eyes were filled with tears that the old woman had to see.

"I'm not part of this family," Kyra whispered.

"You are...in some way."

Well, that wasn't very encouraging. Not the full-on Italian love and hug and reassurance she needed from her very own handpicked *nonna*.

"But you need your own family," Anamaria added.

Kyra blinked, making a tear fall, but she didn't care. The truth of that hurt so much she could hardly breathe. "I don't have one."

Anamaria tilted her head, looking at Kyra with a hint of a smile curling her full lips. "Then make one."

Yeah, just like that. *Thanks, Nonna.* But Kyra didn't do bitter, the way James didn't do fun, so she just smiled and nodded. "Good plan," she murmured. "I'll get right on that."

"You start last night."

She stared at Anamaria, not entirely sure she understood. "I didn't...I mean...I didn't..."

"But you did." Anamaria grinned at her. "And he reached your heart. I see it in your eyes."

"What you see is a lack of sleep. And he's not exactly Mr. Loyal and Trustworthy."

Silent, Anamaria turned and walked toward the sink, slipping her rosary back into her pocket and humming.

Humming? Did she not really comprehend what was about to happen around here? But in a matter of seconds, Anamaria was chopping garlic. Everyone else was gone, busy, and doing their work for the family.

But not *her* family, because she didn't have one.

Chapter Seventeen

James flipped another page of documents, fingering a tiny note that William Hayward had attached when he'd had the paperwork couriered across the ocean. A Post-it Note, pale blue, the same color as Kyra's eyes.

He mumbled a curse and flipped another page, vaguely aware that hours had passed and he hadn't left the room or eaten. All he'd done was go through this mountain of spreadsheets and contracts, trying to fill his brain with numbers, profits, investments, results, and business. Because that way, he didn't have to feel anything.

Wiping his hands over his face, he pushed back from the desk and glanced at the still unmade bed. He could throw himself on those pillows and feel plenty. He could pick up the scent of sex from the night before, inhale a woman he wanted with every fiber of his being, and fall into those Post-it Note blue eyes and *feel*.

He could call her and get her back here, really convincing her that he had no intention of selling the winery. He hadn't told her forcefully enough. She didn't believe him, but he would prove it to her. Prove that he cared.

JAMES

He didn't know how that happened so fast, only that it did. He cared.

A low-grade hum of fear buzzed through him at the thought, and instinctively, he moved back to the desks and documents. James didn't think about it, but when the ache of *feeling* something threatened, there was only one thing to do: work.

When had that started, he suddenly wondered. When had his muscle memory formed so that anything that made him uncomfortable could be erased with the business of *business* instead of the business of *feeling*?

He knew exactly when. Weeks after Mom died, when he'd assumed the job of running that crew and Dad went from a busy guy to a workaholic. When Colin Brannigan finally left his office and came home to the ranch at nine, ten, eleven o'clock at night, six of his seven sons had already crashed. Only James stayed up, having cleaned up the mess of cookies and games and toys left by his brothers. He'd wait to give his daily report, sitting dutifully in front of his father, watching the old man pour a Bushmills 21. Many nights Dad would vent or share some problem, likely because he had no one else to talk to after his beloved best friend had been buried.

James became a young employee and a substitute ear for Colin to fill, and he credited those years with building his appreciation for the fine art of replacing *life* with *work*. Those years taught him how to shove feelings into a file drawer and focus on a good, solid accounting of profits and orderly agendas.

He wove his fingers into his hair and dragged his hand over a head that ached from lack of sleep and food. Again, on instinct, he returned to the papers, and to that one in particular that was bothering him.

He'd already put two calls into Hayward's office to

let him know the Whitehouse Wineries deal was dead, and was frustrated at being told the business manager wasn't around. He hadn't had Hayward on his payroll that long, bringing the man in for the exclusive job of managing certain off-the-mainstream assets, primarily this winery.

The guy should be thrilled with James's news; he'd keep his job longer. If James had sold to Whitehouse, he might have had to let Hayward go. So why didn't he take James's call? He tried again, got the admin with excuses, and flipped through the documents. His gaze settled on the list of distributors, including one named Blue Key Distribution, the one that had to be a US-based company.

Frowning, he remembered asking about that because he knew Villa Pietro wine wasn't distributed in the US. That was one of the "opportunities" that had attracted Whitehouse Wineries. Had Hayward answered? Of course, James didn't know because he'd spent days wrapped up in Kyra Summers and not paying attention to his business.

Stupid.

But Blue Key Distribution was an American company. That might be the perfect place for Kyra, so at least she might still be connected to the wine industry, and she'd be closer to him.

He grunted at how pathetic he was. Grasping at straws to find ways to make her leave the place where she was so happy. Why would he even think that? Still...

He tapped his laptop screen and Googled the distribution company, which was based out of New Jersey. New Jersey? So close to Manhattan, a little voice in his head said. And this company was...currently out of business.

JAMES

What? He clicked through some more, but there it was. Blue Key Distribution had closed down a year ago. Then why was it still showing as a line item on his spreadsheet? And why was money being sent to them?

Someone at Villa Pietro was paying a regular fee to that company, he realized. Sorting through more documents, he found pages of inventory, assets, and accounts payable. There it was, thousands of dollars to BKD, which had to be the same company. A distribution company.

That fell into Bruno's area.

His phone buzzed, and he grabbed it, grateful to see William Hayward's name. "You're not going to believe what I found," James said as he accepted the call.

"You're not going to believe what *I* found," the other man shot back.

"Someone is embezzling from Villa Pietro."

Hayward went silent for a beat. "Are you freaking kidding me?"

"Possibly. Look into payments to a company called Blue Key Distribution and find out where they're coming from and who's writing the check and where they're getting deposited."

"I will, but let me tell you what I'm holding in my hands."

"What?"

"A second offer. Cana Hills Wines just came in at double the price Whitehouse offered."

James dropped back on the chair. "Son of a bitch."

"When it rains, it pours, my friend. They are Whitehouse's biggest competitor, and they want an Italian presence *now*."

"I'm not accepting that."

"Oh hell, I knew you'd say that, Mr. Ethical. And I

know I told you we can't get out of the Whitehouse offer, but I've already got a call in to them to start a bidding war. Are those not your two favorite words?"

"Not exactly. Listen, I'm not taking either offer."

He hooted. "You want more? Of course you do. You're James Brannigan."

James cringed.

"Fine," Hayward said, the thrill of the deal making the man a little too enthusiastic. "I'll open up the offer again, but we have to move fast. Cana Hills is looking at another winery about six miles away from you *this week*. If you accept, they won't even go on the trip."

"Let them. I'm not—"

"Hang on, hang on, hang on. Oh yes. Whitehouse on the other line. This could take a little bit of dancing, but I'm all over it. I'll call you when we have a final offer." Hayward disconnected before James could finish his sentence.

He texted Hayward instead, making it clear he had no intention of selling the winery. Period.

Sighing, he put down the phone and stood up to shower and dress because he had some business of his own to attend to.

An hour later, when James stepped off the Eden Roc shuttle bus outside the gate of the Villa Pietro, his gaze shot immediately to the thick branches of the tree that hung over the path, easily spotting the two undersized guards who protected the property.

When the bus rumbled away, James waited for their high-pitched screech of his name, the swing of a seven-year-old like a little Tarzan, and the full-body bulldozer of a four-year-old's greeting that would nearly knock him over.

But Nico and Gianni didn't move.

JAMES

He rattled the gate, surprised to find it unlocked, and let himself in. As he walked under the tree, he looked up, noticing how still the boys were as they stared down at him.

"Anyone home?" he asked, fighting a smile and bracing for falling children.

"You sell us, Brannigan."

Did he hear that right? His heart fell harder than any child hanging from a tree. She'd told them. She'd told them all, even the littlest Sebastianis. He opened his mouth to tell them they were wrong, but closed it again. They wouldn't understand, and it was Lorenzo who deserved the explanation. Lorenzo and Kyra.

He pointed up at them with a playful warning. "I'm going to be on the bocce court later." Unless they kicked him out. "Who can beat me?"

He waited for Nico's loud cry or Gianni's youthful swagger, but neither of them said a word.

He closed his eyes and headed toward the main house, knocking on the screen door that led into the kitchen. "Nonna?"

The smack of dough on a hard surface was all he heard. No answer to his call. Was the old lady giving him the silent treatment, too? "Nonna?"

The only answer was a muttering in Italian that he suspected was one of many Hail Marys she was reciting. He suspected she wasn't praying for him.

He backed away and rounded the house to the entrance that led to the cellars, pulling the heavy door and stepping down toward the limestone corridor. Men's voices, all Italian, floated up to him, and as he rounded the corner, he cleared his throat to let them know he was there.

Antonio and two of his winemakers looked up from a flatbed of oak barrels and froze.

For a long moment, no one spoke, and James suddenly felt completely and totally out of place. "I was, uh, looking for Kyra," he said, the first thing that came to mind.

Antonio lifted a shoulder. "We are preparing a shipment, *Signor* Brannigan. Very busy."

In other words, get lost.

He backed away, sensing this wasn't the time or place to announce there had been a misunderstanding. Anyway, there hadn't been a misunderstanding; there'd been a lie of omission when he hadn't told them his original plans.

Outside, he took one of the paths that led toward the three stone houses, coming up on a very pregnant Sofia hanging clothes on a line. After clipping a sheet, she paused, rubbing her back and her stomach, letting out a soft moan.

The image was so earthy and moving that he had to stand there for a moment and watch. The delicious scents of lemons mixed with salty, clean air permeated everything, even his heart. The young Italian country woman moving slowly, thick with child and close to delivery, was like some kind of Renaissance painting come to life.

She turned suddenly, sensing him there. "What is it?" she asked in halting English, her breath catching like she was in pain.

"Are you okay, Sofia? Do you need help?"

"No. No help. I'm fine." She scooped up an empty basket and waddled toward the house.

He shook his head, once again feeling like he was somewhere he shouldn't be. But he *owned* the place, damn it.

But not the family. He didn't own the soul of Villa

Pietro. All he had was a piece of paper and some valuable land, and the profits from a small winery. None of that was what made Villa Pietro magic.

As Sofia reached the door, she turned back to him. "Try the lemon grove," she said.

James frowned, not sure he understood.

"The lemon grove." She pointed to the other side of the winery, rubbing her protruding belly with a frown. "Kyra is there."

"Oh, okay. Thanks."

He wasn't going to get anywhere at Villa Pietro unless he had Kyra with him. She might as well own the place, not him. He walked toward the lemon grove he'd visited with Kyra, planning exactly what he'd say to her when he got there.

Please forgive me, it was my mistake, let's kiss and make up and get back to where we were.

How hard could that be? Pretty damn hard if she responded as coldly as the others were.

He reached the edge of the grove and peered into the thick trees. He heard her before he saw her, the sound of her voice already familiar and wonderful to him.

Who was she talking to?

He took a few stealthy steps forward, spotting her on the ground under the tree his parents had claimed for their own. She was on her back, her legs straight up the tree trunk, crossed, her feet bare. She stared up as if challenging one of those fat lemons to fall on her face.

And she talked.

He took a few more steps, about to announce himself when her words reached him.

"Attachments are the issue, aren't they, Colin?" she asked the air.

Colin? She was...talking to his dad?

"That's what hurts people, in the end," she said. "A broken attachment. It's like this branch attached to the tree, getting life from it until..." She reached her arms up and snapped a twig she held. "It breaks and dies."

He just stared at her, silent.

"That's why attachments terrify me, Colin."

Me, too, lemondrop.

"And yet, that's all I want in the whole world. Someone I can count on forever, someone who will put me first, someone who will never break the attachment."

Uncertainty and hope crashed in his chest like two mighty rogue waves trying to discount each other. Could she ever count on him like that? Could he count on her?

She let her arm fall with a thud.

"So, what do you have to tell me, Mr. Brannigan? What should I do?"

James stepped forward. "You should talk to the living Mr. Brannigan, for starters."

She whipped her legs down and shot up with a soft gasp. "What are you doing here?"

"What are *you* doing here?" He looked up into the tree. "Seeing ghosts?"

Color deepened her cheeks. "I needed someone to talk to."

His heart cracked like the twig she'd just snapped. "Talk to me." He closed the space between them and folded right down next to her. "Always talk to me."

She pushed some stray hairs off her face. "Why did you come here?"

He inhaled and let out a long sigh. "I came to tell your family that I'm not selling the winery, but no one wants to talk to me."

JAMES

The shadows of her dimples showed she was fighting a smile. "Honey, they're not my family."

"You know what I mean."

"But they're not, although they will welcome that news. But, I can't go on pretending that they are. I need to leave, James. I need to pack up and move on and do what I do, which is not stay anywhere long enough to grow a root. This is not my home, no matter how badly I want it to be."

"Come to New York. Be with me."

Her eyes flared for a minute. "James."

"Okay, too soon. But maybe don't decide anything for a while?"

Her shoulders sank with relief. "I can't leave when there's a shipment, and tours next week, and Sofia could have her baby any day now. I don't want to miss that."

He took both of her hands in one of his. "I'll stay for a while and you stay for a while and let's see where that takes us."

She held his gaze, her blue eyes locked on his. "What if it takes us nowhere?"

"What if it takes us somewhere neither one of us has ever been before?" Her eyes shuttered closed as if the suggestion hit somewhere too tender. He pulled her closer. "Please give me a chance to prove myself to you." He glanced up the tree. "It's what my dad would tell you to do." He eased her closer and pressed his lips to her ear. "And my mom."

He felt her smile against his cheek. "I was just going to ask her next."

"*Kyraaaaaaaaaaaa!*"

They broke apart at the shriek that cut through the silence of the grove, turning to see Nico and Gianni running toward them, wild-eyed.

"*Il bambino, il bambino, il bambino di Sofia!*"

"Sofia's baby is coming." Kyra pushed up and yanked James with her. "We have to go!"

He didn't argue but scooped Nico into his arms, and each of them took one of Gianni's hands, then they all hustled back to the family.

Chapter Eighteen

By the time Kyra got back from the hospital, it was nearly midnight and there still wasn't a baby. Not a single Sebastiani would leave until there was, though, so Kyra decided to go back and spell James, who had graciously agreed to stay with Nico and Gianni while the entire crew went to the hospital.

She tiptoed into Filippa and Enzo's living room and found the three of them passed out on the sofa. Nico had his head on James's lap. Gianni was curled under his arm. An unfinished board game was on the table in front of them, along with a selection of snacks that told her the kids had done the choosing.

James's head was back, his mouth slack with sleep.

For a long, achy moment, she stared at the sight and let her poor, tired heart *imagine*. What would it be like to come home and find this man and a couple of amazing sons crashed after a night of fun and games? She actually couldn't think of a word that could describe something that amazing, but the longing for it clutched at her belly.

Suddenly, James's head shot up, and his eyes popped open. It took a millisecond for him to get his bearings. "Baby?"

The question damn near folded her in half. "Not yet. But close. I came to relieve the sitter."

"We're..." He started to move his arm but froze when he realized it would wake Gianni. Instead, he slowly repositioned himself, sliding his arm out of place without disturbing the child. Then he put his hands under Nico's head and slipped out from under him, grabbing a pillow for the sleeping child's head.

And Kyra had to stifle an audible swoon.

James put his fingers to his lips and came around the snack- and game-laden table to reach for her. Taking her in his arms, he whispered in her ear, "I played *Gioco Dell'Oca* for four straight hours."

"The goose game?"

"You are looking at a spectacular goose player right here. Although, I let Nico win, because, you know."

She knew. She leaned back, hating that her eyes stung, but too tired to fight it. "You had fun."

"That would be what they call it."

A billionaire playing the goose game...and liking it. "It's a breakthrough."

He kissed her forehead. "They're great kids, in any language."

"You're a great..." She almost said *father*. "Guy for helping us out in a pinch."

"No problem. Is Sofia okay? Everything normal?"

She nodded. "Just first-baby slow. Thank you for staying with the boys. It meant the world to me to be there tonight, and I would have stayed with the kids if you hadn't been here."

"Did you tell everyone?" he asked. "Did you tell them I'm not selling the winery?"

"I did. And they are relieved and happy and..." *They all want us to get married.* She tamped down that particular truth, because it would ruin the perfection of this quiet, somehow intimate moment.

"And they believe you?"

"Shouldn't they?" she challenged.

His eyes narrowed at her. "Stop it," he said, only half teasing. "Do you want anything?"

"To help you put these two in bed," she said. "Let's do Nico first. He's lighter."

"I got them," he assured her. "I just didn't want them to wake up and be scared because they were with some strange guy they were told to hate this afternoon."

"I didn't tell them to hate you," she said.

"Then they figured it out on their own." He turned and looked at the boys, his expression softening the way it did when he talked about his mother. "But I disavowed them of that notion."

She smiled at that. "How?"

"I have six younger brothers. Do you even have to ask?"

She gestured to the remnants of candied apples and chocolate cake on the table. "I thought you were the one who kept law and order."

Laughing softly, he went back to the sofa and gently scooped up a limp Nico. "How do you think I kept it? Bribery. Where does this one go?"

"Their room is back here." She led him to the hall and turned on the night-light, walking to turn back Nico's bedcovers. James laid him down and then went to get Gianni while Kyra tucked Nico in and brushed a lock of dark hair off his sweet, sleeping face.

When they had Gianni in bed, too, both of them stood in the middle of the dark room, surrounded by the sounds of sleeping children and a house wrapped in love. Once again, Kyra felt an ache she couldn't even describe clutch at her.

"I missed you, lemondrop," he whispered, embracing her.

She laid her head against his chest and listened to his heart. "But you had fun."

"It was like old times for me." He stroked her head and turned her a little, looking from one boy to the other. "They remind me so much of Finn and Knox when they were that age. A little annoying, a little goofy, a lot of pure boy. At the risk of being completely cheeseball, I have to tell you that tonight took me back to…to before."

At the hitch in his voice, she looked up at him. "And how'd that feel?"

"Familiar. Good. Right. Like…like…"

"*La famiglia è tutto*?" she suggested.

"Exactly." He curled an arm around her. "Are we going to stay here and wait for baby news?"

"Well, I am. You can go back to the hotel. We can call the shuttle for you."

He shot her a *get real* look. "I saw some wine in a jug in there."

"I'm sure you did, and it's the good stuff, if I know Enzo and Filippa."

"I could use a slug. C'mon. I'll kick your ass in the goose game. I don't care how cute you are." He kissed her nose and led her out. "Although you are pretty damn cute."

The next morning, after a great breakfast and a family celebration that baby Marcella had been born at 4:25 a.m. and mom and daughter were doing well, James endured another motor scooter ride behind Kyra down the mountain. He was getting braver, closing his eyes only when a truck rumbled by inches away or she swerved around a blind corner. He held on to his girl, inhaled the fresh smell of the Amalfi Coast, and planned exactly what he was going to do when they got to his suite. He had to make his point absolutely clear.

Once inside the cool suite, he took her hand and led her back to his bedroom.

"No dawdling for conversation, I see," she mused.

"We can converse. But I have something to show you."

"What?"

"My work area."

"The fun never stops with you."

He just laughed and took her past the bed to the mountain of paperwork still on the massive desk that ran the length of the wall. "I want you to watch this."

She crossed her arms and nodded. "Okay."

He picked up the original offer letter from Whitehouse Wineries and tore it from top to bottom, earning a surprised look. Then he let the torn papers flutter into the trash. "And the rest of this?" He gestured toward all the documents that had been growing since this deal started. "Watch."

With one long, smooth move, he swiped everything off the desk onto the floor, clearing the wood. All that was left was his laptop, which he closed and slid into the top drawer. "There. No work. How's that look to you?" he asked, unable to hide his smile of pride at the completely empty desk.

"Like a really good surface for…" She slipped between him and the desk, leaning back on the wood surface and looking up at him with a flirtatious glint in her eyes. "Work."

"That's what desks are usually for."

Slowly, she scooted onto the top, a smile pulling at her lips. "Very hard work," she said with a tease that instantly got a reaction low in his gut.

Or was that his damn phone? Reaching into his pocket, he pulled out his buzzing cell and puffed a disgusted breath at William Hayward's name. "One of my business managers."

She held out her hand. "Give me the phone."

Lifting his brows, he complied, and she tapped the screen, holding up one finger to keep him quiet. Sitting further back on the empty surface of the desk, she put the phone to her ear. "Good morning, Mr. Brannigan's office. How may I help you?"

He smiled at her official voice, but the smile faded as she flicked the first button of her top. At the same time, she kicked off one of her sandals and put her bare foot right on his crotch. Which was already growing.

"I'm so sorry, Mr. Hayward. Mr. Brannigan is…" She unbuttoned the rest and revealed a lacy yellow bra. "In the middle of a very important meeting."

He could hear the man's voice coming through the phone, with his usual sense of urgency, while Kyra used her free hand to pull her skirt up her thighs.

James's mouth went bone-dry.

"I understand how important your call is, Mr. Hayward, but Mr. Brannigan is…" She spread her legs and gave him a shot of sweet yellow panties. "Up to his…" She crooked a finger and invited him closer. "Eyeballs in work right now."

Fighting the urge to laugh mixed with the strongest desire to kiss her, James slid between her legs, letting his hard-on hit right on the butter-yellow target between her legs.

Hayward's voice got louder, insisting that Kyra interrupt James, but she tipped her head back, offering her neck and breasts to James. He pressed his lips on her skin and grazed her silky thighs with both hands.

"I will certainly relay your message to Mr. Brannigan," she cooed, reaching her hand into James's pants and closing her fingers around his erection. "Thank you so much for calling. I know how *hard*…" She winked at him and stroked. "It can be to get a *hold* of him."

He had to press his lips into her skin to keep from making a sound.

"All right, then," she finished. "Good-bye. Have a lovely day, Mr. Hayward." She rocked into him, letting her wet panties slide over his ridge. "Oh, I am. Thank you."

She thumbed the phone, set it on the desk, and gave it a good push to the side.

"You…" He worked his way to her mouth. "Have the job."

"Title, please?"

"President of Fun."

She gave a victorious hoot and pulled him into her. "You know what I need to be happy at work?"

"A big…" He slipped his finger behind the silk and found the sweet, wet center of her. "Juicy…" He circled her center. "Raise?"

"And a very private meeting with my boss."

"We can arrange that." He held her gaze as he grabbed his wallet and retrieved a condom and pushed off his pants. "On the desk, lemondrop?"

"Only if you've never made love to anyone on a desk before."

"I haven't," he said quickly, and it was the truth. "In fact, I've never…"

"What?"

Made *love*, he thought. It was always sex. Always...meaningless. Always a distraction and release and escape. But not this. "I've never made love to anyone like you."

"We *have* firmly established I'm not your type."

He worked his way between her legs again, this time ready to get all the way inside her. "I don't care about types," he said gruffly as he slipped the tip of his erection into her.

She sucked in a breath and eased him closer.

"I care about you," he whispered as he slid into her.

Her eyes widened, either from the admission or the sensation.

"I care so much about you, Kyra Summers." He made the confession into a kiss, but that didn't mean it was any less true. "I only want to be with you. Only. You."

She moaned and took him deeper, arching her back and wrapping her legs around his hips. "Only...you," she repeated, closing her eyes and letting her head fall back as he thrust completely into her.

James gripped her with two hands, closing his eyes, letting his body say everything he didn't know how to say.

He wanted her. He adored her. He...he...

Oh yeah. He loved her.

He didn't even know what love felt like, but it must feel like...*this*. Precious. Perfect. Hot and achy and like he died and went to heaven.

They clung to each other as they let go and came together, groaning with pleasure, sharing the sensations, completely lost in the exquisite connection they shared.

When it was over, Kyra slumped against him. "You do your best work at a desk, boss."

He groaned at the name. "I have good help." He held her against him and turned his head to the side, his gaze landing on the pile of papers he'd dumped so unceremoniously on the floor.

On top of the stack was one page with that blue Post-it Note that reminded him of her eyes. He made a mental note to call his assistant in New York and have her deliver a few packs to this suite.

Because when he told Kyra Summers that he loved her, he would do it in a way that left no doubt in her mind.

There was certainly no doubt in his.

Chapter Nineteen

"James?" Kyra turned under the soft Egyptian cotton sheets, still not used to waking up with him even though she had every morning for days. She hadn't slept at the winery once, but they'd visited in between sightseeing, beach-going, and...this.

Wonderful hours in bed spent laughing and talking and making love. Wanting more of all of that, Kyra patted the pillow next to her and frowned because it was empty. "James?"

She waited for him to call back, either from the kitchen or living area, maybe the balcony or bathroom. But the suite that had started to feel like home was quiet.

Pushing up, she brushed some hair off her face and blinked into the early morning light. Where was—

Her hand landed on a paper on the sheet, and she turned to peer at it, frowning at a small pink heart-shaped...Post-it Note.

Oh. Her own heart swelled with affection as she peeled the paper off the sheet and read the words.

Get dressed for a walk. Have I told you lately how beautiful you are? With a hand-drawn heart. Pushing out of bed, she walked into the bathroom to brush her teeth and found another sticky note on the mirror.

JAMES

After you're dressed, go to the balcony. And you make me smile. With a smiley face.

A smiley face! He was so not a smiley face kind of guy that this one put a big grin on her own face.

She followed the orders and walked through an empty suite to find another heart-shaped note on the glass-topped table where they'd shared many meals while watching the sunset.

Stop by the front desk. Spread your sunshine to everyone. With a sketch of the sun, complete with rays. They were hand-drawn emojis, she realized, and for some reason, that touched her enough to fill her eyes.

Sighing, she made her way to the lobby and reception area, where Rosa, one of the friendly staff, greeted her in Italian and, without being asked, held out a pink Post-it Note heart. "He's a nice man," she said.

"Yeah," Kyra agreed. "Very sweet."

"He needed help with some Italian." She leaned forward. "He's a...how do you say? A keeping one."

A keeper. "He sure is." She took the note and read it, unable to keep from letting out a little moan of delight.

Head to the scalinatella. Did you wear your signature color? Was that a lemon he'd sketched?

Laughing, she glanced down at the yellow skirt and white top she wore. Of course she had. "Guess I'm going down to the beach," she said, waving to Rosa and heading out into the warm morning sunshine.

When had he done all this, she wondered. And why?

Her heart tripped as she darted across the street and turned the corner at a coffee shop.

"*Buongiorno!*" a waiter called out as he cleaned an outside table.

Spread your sunshine, she thought. She gave him a cheery wave. "It *is* a good morning," she practically sang. Following the main road as it snaked down through the mountainside town, she paused, looking out over the top of a massive pergola carpeted in purple bougainvillea. But one pink paper heart stood out among the flowers. Plucking it, she read, *Down the stairs, lemondrop. I can't wait to kiss you.* And he has drawn lips!

James Brannigan, who knew you were so romantic? For a moment, she looked up to the deep-blue sky, eyeing the one big cotton-ball cloud that hung over the Mediterranean like a guest who refused to leave. Were his parents up there? Watching with pride as their son finally found…

She swallowed the word.

She couldn't bear to say it. It was too soon. Too scary. Too perfect. But she knew what she felt in her heart and could only hope he felt the same.

Turning the first corner, she looked around, the whole world somehow brighter and more beautiful than it ever was. A young man on a corner strummed a guitar, singing in Italian. The smells of espresso and baked bread teased her nose. Above her, more bougainvillea shaded the path that was as much a walkway as it was stairs, all leading down to the jewel of Positano—the beach.

And James.

As she reached the porcelain store, she slowed her step, somehow knowing he must have left a note for her. Sure enough, stuck to the lemon-decorated platter hanging by the open doors, another pink heart.

All the way to the beach. I'm waiting for you. He'd drawn a stick figure of a man waving.

She giggled at the sheer joy of it, the happiness, the fun.

JAMES

He remembered her silly story about the Post-it Notes. He remembered and cared and made such an effort.

She'd changed James in these days and weeks. He'd arrived a hardened businessman with his only concern the bottom line, and today he was playful, romantic, silly, and used hand-drawn emojis.

She loved that about him.

She loved…him.

"Oh, Kyra. Slow your crazy self," she whispered as she finally reached the point where the long stairs opened up to a wide area of shops, restaurants, and the promenade that ran along the umbrella-dotted beach. All around her was beauty. On either side, reaching to the sky, the mountains were dotted with pastel-colored homes and ribboned with streets that James thought were so dangerous.

Out on the water, a large tourist boat was pulling out from the harbor, headed to Amalfi or Ravello or Capri. Pizza makers were already at work, and everywhere there were tourists and locals, waking up and taking in paradise.

And there, leaning against the wall, looking right at her, was James.

Her James. Her love.

Even from a hundred feet away, she could see him smile, his hands in the pockets of his shorts, his T-shirt stretched over broad shoulders. He lifted a hand to wave her down just as her purse buzzed with a call.

Well, it couldn't be James, because she could see him and he wasn't on the phone. In fact, he hadn't touched his phone in days. It stayed right on the corner of the desk in the bedroom where she'd pushed it. When his phone vibrated, he ignored it, telling her she was more important than work.

And she should do the same thing now, but habit made her pull it out of her bag and see the caller ID was Villa Pietro. It was early, but it could be Anamaria. Or one of the kids. Or something with the new baby.

She tapped the phone, ready to tell whoever it was that she'd call back until she heard the crack in Elena's voice.

"*Cara. Cara*! You must come."

She froze in her spot. "What's the matter?"

"It's over! It's over! Everything is over. The *polizia* take Bruno!"

"The police?" She gasped and covered her other ear to be sure she understood. "What? Bruno was arrested?"

Elena sobbed. "And the people! These…these Cana people! They are everywhere!"

She couldn't breathe, lifting her head to get air and her gaze falling on James, who watched her. "What do you mean, Elena? Who are the Cana people?"

"They buy Villa Pietro! From James! They pay millions and millions of dollar and tell us we have one week—one week, *Cara*!—and they go into the cellar and start turning off the equipment and then in the office, looking at papers. It's like they've taken over."

She was dizzy, the sun beating down, the words incomprehensible. Except for one. *They've taken over.* That phrase was…familiar.

"This man he says we have to leave," Elena cried. "He has paper and legal stuff and words I do not understand like…like allowances and dismissal and *compensation metrics*."

Oh yes. All words she'd heard throughout her whole childhood. The vocabulary of a *closer*.

"I'll be right there," she managed to say, looking up to see James striding toward her.

JAMES

He had to know. He *had* to. He owned the business, he called the shots, he made every decision. He had to know. And if he didn't, then—

"What's the matter?" he asked.

What was the matter was that he'd always do this to people. If not to her, then some other happy person who suddenly had their life upended. That's what he was, that's what he did. And she hated it. Eventually, she'd hate him.

She shook her head, her throat too thick to talk.

"Kyra, what's wrong?"

She lifted her hand, full of pink Post-It Notes. "Here." She shoved them at him. "Here's your pink slip."

He just stared at her as her phone, still in her hand, vibrated again. "What are you talking about?"

"I just can't...believe in you."

Even in the sun, she could see him pale, stepping back as though she'd smacked him with the words. "Kyra..."

"Maybe you know, maybe you don't. But whatever, it's you and what you are, and I don't want to spend my life with someone like that."

He blinked in shock. Probably because she'd said *spend my life* when they sure as hell hadn't talked about anything like that. And they never would. But if this didn't lead there, then where did this romantic scavenger hunt lead at all? It was all she wanted and...

"Please," he said, his voice strained as he reached her. "Kyra."

Fear rocked her right down to the soles of her feet. Was she worthy of an attachment like he was promising? Was he capable of giving it? Her phone buzzed again and again and again.

"My family needs me," she whispered, turning away and running back up the long *scalinatella*, leaving Positano and James and her notes and all that hope behind.

James stood with the sun on his face, feeling nothing but ice in his veins. What the holy hell just happened? He watched the yellow and white frock disappear into the crowd, past the beachfront restaurants and stores, and…away.

She left him. She *left* him for no good reason and with no chance to hear the three words that he was so ready to say to her.

Women leave. Joyous, bright, warm, *fun* women leave. When would he learn that lesson?

Swallowing the thought, he looked down at the handful of ridiculous notes he'd gotten up in the middle of the night to write and paid an employee of the Eden Roc a small fortune to plant.

What a foolish, inane waste of time and money and feelings.

As he passed a trash can, he tossed in the notes and made his way back up the long and windy stairs and path that was the only way back to his hotel. Tourists jostled him, and vendors smiled at him, and the sights and smells and sounds of magical Positano pressed so hard it was a wonder he could drag himself back up to the main street.

There, two scooters whizzed by and nearly knocked him over, and he didn't even flinch. He rounded the last corner and looked up at the stacked balconies of the Eden Roc, bathed in purple flowers and more sunshine.

JAMES

It was time to go home, he thought. He'd call his assistant, arrange for the plane to be ready, and get back to work, which was life. Staying here one more day was just stupid.

The woman at the desk looked surprised when he walked into the cool, dimly-lit lobby. "*Signor* Brannigan. We were not expect—"

He waved off the greeting and marched to the elevator, head down. When the doors opened, he was surprised to see Mario, one of the hotel employees, standing outside his suite, his arms crossed, his expression serious.

Was Kyra in there?

His heart literally soared as he hustled closer.

"*Signor* Brannigan," the man said. "Your guest is here insisted on entering."

He frowned, both at the announcement and the strange note in Mario's voice. "Guest?"

Mario paled. "You were expecting *Signor* Hayward?" He handed him a business card with William Hayward's name and the Brannigan Capital logo, with James's own handwriting on the card that said *Permission to grant access*, and his signature. At least it looked like his signature.

What the hell? "He's in there?"

"Is that all right, *Signor*? He insisted."

"Yeah, it's fine." He headed inside. "He's an insistent kind of guy." And intrusive, James thought, but that made him an excellent project manager for things James didn't want to think or worry about. Like the winery.

Was that why he was here?

It had to be. James had hired him shortly after Dad died, handing over the management of the winery to a man who had an impressive résumé managing remote businesses. It was so much easier than even thinking about Villa Pietro, which James hadn't wanted to do.

But now...now there was no one in the entryway or living room or on the balcony, then—

Hayward bounded out of the bedroom, inhaling sharply when he saw James.

"What are you doing here?" they asked each other in perfect unison.

"James, I...I..." Color rose to his angular features, reddening him from a sharp chin to dark blond roots. He took a shallow breath, which caught in his throat. "I needed to talk to you."

"In my bedroom?"

"I thought you might still be asleep."

Seriously? Frowning, James's gaze slipped behind the man, falling on the unmade bed and the sight of Kyra's undergarments left in haste on the floor. "Well, that was an intrusion," he said, taking a step to push by him so he could close the bedroom door.

"Wait." He snagged James's arm, sending a shot of adrenaline and anger through him.

"I will not wait." James yanked free and walked to the door, blinking in surprise at the mess on his desk. Days ago, the maid had picked up the papers he'd swept off and piled them into a neat stack on the corner. But now, they were spread out and messed up and...

"Were you going through my work?" James asked, incredulity lifting his voice.

"I was looking for the original offer."

"You could have asked." James pulled the door and spun around to Hayward, who was stuffing something in a suit jacket pocket and inching toward the front door. "What the hell are you doing?" he demanded.

"Look, James, I just closed an amazing deal and you made seven figures and the first is certainly not a one."

He took another backward step. "You continue your vacation, and I'll—"

"You *what*?" James had to restrain himself from leaping on the guy. "You sold the winery?"

"For more than twice the original offer." He had the audacity to sound *smug* about that. "It's all done."

"Done?" Fury punched through the fog that had hovered over him all the way up here. "What is done?"

"The sale, the turnover and, thank God for your keen eye, the arrest of Bruno Sebastiani, who was stealing a tidy sum from your coffers, my friend."

He actually couldn't move, because if he did, he'd throttle this son of a bitch and couldn't be held accountable for the outcome. Instead, James gritted his teeth and got right into Hayward's face.

"Whatever the hell unauthorized decision you made better be just as easily undone."

"Undone?" His eyes widened. "Millions, James," he replied in a low, slow voice. "I just made you millions. You wanted to sell the place, and I did, and I made you millions, which is all you ever wanted. What the hell is wrong with you?"

"What is wrong with *you*? It wasn't yours to sell! I told you not to sell the winery. Who signed the deal?"

"I did, with the power of attorney you gave me a year ago when you handed this business to me to manage for you. I've signed your name a lot of times. You just never paid attention before."

James narrowed his eyes. "Power of attorney doesn't give you the authority to sell it."

"It gives me the authority to sign on your behalf, and you've been so…" He tipped his head toward the bedroom door and lifted his brows. "Distracted, if you know what I mean."

Ire ripped through him.

"I understand when there is a good piece of ass, it's tough to fo—"

James slammed him against the wall with one rough push. "Shut up."

Hayward stayed frozen, fighting for composure as James held him. "She lives with that family. You know they just used her to change your mind about selling. You know that, don't you?"

His fist tightened, ready to throw a punch right across this bastard's jaw. "I'd tell you to leave, Hayward, but we have to undo the damage you've done."

He choked softly. "You really don't know what they had her do, do you? Well, I do. Bruno told me everything."

James drew back in shock, just enough for Hayward to find that composure and straighten his jacket.

"They forced her to get 'cozy' with you so you wouldn't sell."

"You don't know what you're talking about."

"I don't? Did she not coerce you into doing nothing but sightseeing for days and days? Well." He snorted. "Sightseeing and sex, I guess."

"Shut up!" James yelled in his face. "And get the hell out. I don't need you to fix things. You're fired, and you're—"

"How can you be so stupid?" Hayward ground out. "I mean, how can you have your head up your ass so far you don't see that and still manage to make a billion dollars?"

"I'm going to put your head up your ass with my fist if you don't get out now."

He had his shit together now, James could tell. Stepping away from where James had him trapped against the wall, he pulled his cuffs and surreptitiously pushed that piece of paper deeper into his pocket.

"What is—"

"They planned the whole thing, you know," Hayward said. "She and that Bruno guy are an item. You do know that, don't you? Hell, he gets a boner just talking about her."

Blood drained from James's head.

"They're sending money to a bogus account in New Jersey to make it look like they're paying a distributor there that's been defunct for a year. From there, who knows where the money goes? The whole plan would blow up in their faces when you sold, and they knew it. So the family dreamed up this thing to make her 'get cozy' with you. They sent her to distract you and then convince you—however she thought necessary—not to sell the place. They were all in on it, even the old lady. James, don't look at me that way. It's an exact quote from Bruno while we were interrogating him."

"You *interrogated* him? And who's *we*?"

"I had to find out who was embezzling, and I have my spies in Naples. He showed up there, and…and I did, too."

"Did you hurt him?" James asked, his chest tightening at the thought.

"Do you care? You're both boning the same woman."

James threw the punch. Hard. It was like his fist had a mind of its own as it slammed right into Hayward's jaw and sent him tumbling back. "You're lying," James said.

The other man held up both hands. "Whatever, man. Believe whatever. The winery's sold. The Cana Hills people are already up there moving into the cellars and looking at the equipment and giving the instructions to the family on how to get out. Their closers are up there."

Closers. No wonder she ran away from him.

"You bastard." James gave him another push. "Get the hell out."

As Hayward tripped backward, James reached into the man's jacket pocket and whipped out the paper.

"Hey! That's mine."

"From my office." James flipped it open and instantly recognized the spreadsheet. The words Blue Key Distribution jumped out at him, the numbers next to the company's name in the tens of thousands. "What is this?" he demanded.

"Nothing. A duplicate of something that I found in your office."

James glared at him. "*Bruno* is embezzling?" he challenged. "Or you are?"

He paled just enough for James to know the truth.

"Something you could hide once you sold the company, right?" James pressed. "No wonder you were in such a rush."

Hayward tried to snag the paper away, but James jerked it back, the truth smacking him, making so much sense, as the truth so often did. "I'll pay you back."

James tossed the paper to the side because he needed both hands. "You lying son of a bitch, you stole the money and let someone else take the blame." He shoved Hayward's shoulders again, pushing him to the wall and getting both hands on his collar. "You stole it and you knew I'd figure it out as soon as I paid attention so you sold the winery." He slammed his head against the wall, lifting the man's narrow frame a few inches off the floor. "Guess what? I'm paying attention, William."

"J-J-James…please. This isn't like you."

"Damn right it isn't." He knocked him against the wall again, thudding his head.

JAMES

"*Signor* Brannigan?" Mario called from outside. "Are you all right?"

He lifted Hayward a little higher, taking unholy pleasure in the man's fear and misery. Too much pleasure, he realized. And he had more important business to take care of than this clown.

"Call the *polizia*, Mario!" he yelled. "And send more staff up here! I've caught a thief."

Three staff members entered the suite instantly, already out there and waiting.

Hayward glanced at them, then looked at James with abject terror. "We don't need to call the police, James. Let's just handle this like men."

"Yeah, let's." He jammed his knee into Hayward's nuts, and the guy crumbled with a groan. In one move, James snagged the paperwork, stuffed it into his pocket, and brushed off his hands. "I need the hotel van," he said to Mario.

His eyes widened. "It's not here, sir. If you wait, I'll call you a cab."

Wait? He couldn't wait. "I need a car. Now."

"You can have my scooter," Mario said, reaching into his pocket for keys. "It's parked across the street at the stand. A yellow Vespa. But I don't have a helmet."

A yellow Vespa with no helmet. Perfect. "Thanks." He snagged the keys, ran down the steps without waiting for an elevator, and charged out the front door to cross the street just as a huge truck barreled by and nearly ran him down.

He didn't care. He found the bike, threw himself onto it, twisted the ignition, and headed up the mountain to his winery and his woman.

He was not going to lose either one.

Chapter Twenty

It was like a nightmare. The worst kind of nightmare when you knew it couldn't be true but everything was so *real*. The family was spread around the winery, along with a group of Americans who seemed so foreign, it was hard to believe she'd ever called these people countrymen.

They weren't mean or overbearing or even heartless, but they had a job to do and they did it with speed, efficiency, and zero personal warmth.

She almost wanted to ask if they knew Jane Summers, because surely these types all hung out in the bar at the national closer conferences. But she didn't. Instead, she translated for everyone, since this brilliant American company that was synonymous with cheap wine had sent a crew that didn't include a single Italian speaker.

So from the moment Kyra returned and tried to process what was happening, she'd been bouncing from place to place, helping facilitate communication. Somehow, she translated conversations between the idiots who'd just been handed the greatest gift in the world and the family she loved.

Antonio had gone with one of them to the cellars,

assuring her his English was good enough to talk to the man who claimed to be another enologist, and asked Kyra to stay with Sofia, who was fighting tears and rocking the baby. They sat at the table with Filippa, who'd lost all shred of control of Nico and Gianni. The two women were talking with another woman named Alexis, who had beady green eyes, flat dishwater-blond hair, and thick lips she chewed on when Sofia rattled on in Italian.

"We will take care of you," Alexis said, looking at Kyra. "Please explain we will take care of the family with fair compensation and corporate assistance to find housing."

"Housing?" Kyra shot back. "They don't need housing. They need a *home*."

She shifted in her seat and gnawed that lip some more. "Well, I would appreciate if you could explain that it is my job with Cana Hills Wines to arrange for a transitional lifestyle to any former employees who require provisional benefits during the management change."

Kyra's stomach turned. "Here's what I'll translate," she said to the woman. "I'll tell her some bitch is going to find you an apartment since they just forced you and *your newborn baby* out of the home that your husband's family has lived in for fifty years. That okay?"

Alexis stood. "Ma'am, I realize this is an emotional tipping point for everyone, but my title is clear. I'm an agent of change, and I will assist all of the employees—"

"They're family!" Kyra exclaimed. "Not employees. And agent of change is just another euphemism for destroyer of lives!"

She whipped around as the back door opened and Lorenzo came in with Bruno, who looked like a shell of a man. The minute they walked in, Anamaria popped out of the pantry, her rosary wrapped around her fingers and at her lips.

"Bruno!" All of the women in the room exclaimed in unison, including Kyra. His gaze landed on her, raw pain in his eyes.

"I told you, *Cara*," he said softly.

A whimper caught in her throat as she crossed the kitchen to reach him. "Yes, you did, Bruno."

"They are saying I did something I didn't," he said vehemently. "They tried to pay me to say I did it."

Lorenzo shook his head and swore in Italian.

"Did you admit anything?" Kyra asked.

"No, but this man had paperwork with my name on it, and I was very confused."

"What man?" she asked.

"Someone named Hayward."

Kyra's eyes closed, reeling as the last nail went into James's coffin. He was dead to her. Forever and ever dead to her. "His business manager. James must have been playing us all along."

"Well, I told him we were playing right back," Bruno said.

Everyone in the room looked at him, confused, certain they hadn't understood his English, but Kyra had. "You told him what?"

"That two could play his game. That you got 'cozy' to get information and—"

"You told him that?" Kyra put her hand on her chest. Now he'd think...oh, what did it matter? It was over anyway.

At the table, Alexis the family destroyer cleared her throat. "Excuse me, but could we get back to these forms?"

Kyra glared at her. "You know what you need to do, Alexis? Get lost. Get the hell out of this kitchen, which is not a conference room. It's a home. And this is a family. And we don't need a professional closer to help us transition through anything. We are a family, and we can do it without your help. Go." Kyra pointed to the door. "Go find one of your American friends and get a glass of wine and leave us alone. We have family things to attend to. Go!"

The woman looked down at her papers and sniffed. "I'll find the others," she said, as if it were her own idea.

When she walked out, Kyra practically fell into Anamaria's outstretched arms, the two of them embracing.

"*Cara, Cara,*" the old woman said, patting her back. "Hush, child."

Kyra closed her eyes and gave in to the ministrations just as a loud shriek came from outside, high-pitched and wild.

"It's the boys," Filippa said, standing up. "I'll get th—"

"*Braaaaaannnnigan!*" Gianni hollered, his little feet pounding the stone with the same force that Kyra's heart suddenly hit her ribs.

He was here? He had the audacity to come here?

Everyone in the kitchen stared at her, their faces registering the same shock she felt. "I didn't know he was coming," she said.

Bruno took a deep breath, his nostrils flaring. "I'll handle him."

Anamaria knocked her knuckles against his shoulder. "You hide."

"Hide?"

"And you." She pointed a gnarled finger in Kyra's

face. "We get the truth out of him. He sees you, he lie."

"What truth? There is no—"

The door smacked open, and the boys ran inside. "Brannigan on a scooter with no helmet!" Nico said, beaming with pride for his tattletale skills.

But Kyra almost fell over. "He rode a scooter? Himself? With no helmet? Up the mountain?"

Anamaria was already pushing Bruno toward the pantry, and she got a grip on Kyra's arm. "You stay with him. Keep him hidden. Hurry!"

She pushed them both toward the walk-in pantry, and Kyra let her. It would be much easier to hide. She didn't want to look into his endless brown eyes and remember how soft and sweet and tender his gaze could be...when he was making love.

She followed Bruno in, planning to stay long enough to hear what lies he spread and then, when he thought he had all the control, she'd come out and confront him.

"You keep him here!" Anamaria ordered, pointing at Bruno but talking to Kyra. Then, to him, she said, "You in enough trouble. Keep it shut." She reached into her pocket and pulled out a garlic clove and handed it to Kyra. "In his mouth if he talk."

And she left them there, one little light overhead, the smell of basil and tomatoes permeating the stuffy air.

"Excuse me!" a man's voice boomed, and Kyra got closer to the door to listen, but she knew instantly that wasn't James. It was one of the Cana Hills people—the guy in charge, she guessed. Henry Wassel or Wesley. Weasel, she decided.

"They kicked me out!" Oh, that was fat-lipped Alexis.

"I'm getting nothing from this Antonio guy."

A new voice. Kyra glanced at Bruno and whispered,

JAMES

"That's the fake winemaker named Jackson or Franklin or Johnson. Some president."

He just looked at her, still seething, but quiet.

"People, we need your cooper—"

The kitchen door flew open again, and every sound in the room stopped. Dead silence. Kyra pressed to the door.

"Where's Kyra?" James's voice was not angry, but flat, serious, like he meant business.

"She not here," Anamaria said, no doubt squeezing that rosary and begging forgiveness for the lie.

"You can leave now," James said.

Who could leave now?

"We're not going anywhere," Weasel replied.

"I'm James Brannigan, and I'm ordering you and you and you off this property. I own it, and you are not welcome."

A chill danced up Kyra's spine as she glanced at Bruno, who drew back, surprised.

"Mr. Brannigan," Weasel said. "May I call you James?"

"No, you may pack up your stuff, get in your car, and leave this property."

"You're no longer the owner." That was the president guy. "Here's the contract."

"Give it to me."

She heard footsteps, paper, and the silence of a whole lot of people holding their breath.

"Uh-huh, yes, I see," James said, and Kyra could picture him reading. "Excuse me for a moment. May I use your stove, Nonna?"

Kyra put her hand to her lips, the use of the nickname like a balm on her broken heart.

"He's cooking the books?" Bruno whispered, as rapt at the drama unfolding as she was.

"I think he's…"

A gasp went through the room, loud enough to be heard in the pantry, and the acrid smell of smoke drifted under the pantry door.

"Very dramatic, Mr. Brannigan," President Guy said. "But I have a copy at the Cana Hills offices and with our attorney and another with your business manager."

"Yes, my business manager. Then you'll be interested in this, a document that proves he's been embezzling from Villa Pietro for at least eight months, and you know what that means?"

No one spoke, but Bruno put his hand over his mouth and looked at Kyra.

"He's currently under arrest in Positano, so any document he signed is null and void, and I am rescinding any agreement he signed to sell this winery to you."

His voice rose until he was yelling, even though the room was silent. "Is that clear?" he asked, louder still. "Is that clear to *everyone who is listening*?"

A few people murmured, and some shoes scuffed, and a laptop closed, and some more people mumbled that they had to get some things from the office before they left.

"Did everyone hear that?" James repeated, his voice booming now.

And then Kyra knew. She knew exactly what he was doing, exactly why his voice was raised.

"Because I want everyone in this house and family and hiding in the pantry to know that this winery is owned by me right now, but not for long. I am selling it."

She froze, sucking in a breath, closing her eyes as her whole body felt like she just fell off a cliff and hit bottom. In the kitchen, voices rose, in English and Italian, soft cries and loud reactions.

JAMES

"You are?" Lorenzo's voice rose above the others.

"To you," James said. "For one dollar. Today. Villa Pietro belongs to you and your family, Lorenzo. And I will continue to invest in it and help finance the operation as long as there is a Sebastiani here."

"Oh." Anamaria whimpered.

"James!" The cry was in unison, from every other person in the room. Well, every Italian person in the room. She suspected the Cana Hills people were stunned into silence.

"He's giving us the winery?" Bruno whispered.

"Yes," Kyra said, blinking back tears. "I think so."

"I only have one stipulation, Lorenzo," James said. "One condition, one…thing I have to have to be happy."

Kyra pressed her hand to her mouth.

"Whatever you want," Lorenzo replied.

"When my wife and I return here, we always have a place to stay."

His wife? His…*wife*?

"James," she whispered, her hand trembling as she tried to open the door.

She stepped out of the pantry into the kitchen, vaguely aware of the reactions of everyone in the room but not seeing any of them. Just James, standing stone-still, staring at her, the hint of a smile almost covering up the fear and hope and, oh God, love in his eyes.

"That is, if you'll ever leave this place," he whispered. "If not, I'll just move here so you never have to leave if you don't want to."

Slowly, she came closer, her gaze locked on him. "I'll go where you are, James. And that will be home."

He reached out and took her hand. "I've been trying to tell you something all day."

She smiled. "It *has* been a challenge today."

"Anything good is worth fighting for," he said. "Worth writing notes for. Worth nearly dying on a scooter for. Worth kicking out scum and fighting the bad guys for."

She tightened her grip on his fingers. "And worth giving up the winery for?"

He nodded to Lorenzo. "It's in good hands. But I came to say something else, too, and I'm going to say it."

She nodded, lost and happy and bubbling with joy. "Yes?"

He searched her face, his gaze intent and pure and true. "I love you, Kyra."

She bit her lip. "I love you, too, James."

For a long time, he didn't say anything, then he turned to Anamaria. "Nonna, do you have a knife? A good strong one that can carve anything."

"Anything?" she asked.

"Anything…like a tree."

"A tree?"

Kyra blinked, and a tear rolled down her face. "A lemon tree," she whispered.

He slipped his arm around her, took a chef's knife from Anamaria, and looked at all of them. "Exactly. Now, if you'll excuse us, Kyra and I need to go carve something in a lemon tree."

Epilogue

"Brannigan!" Nico barreled out onto the bocce court, bounding onto James's back and wrecking any chance of a decent toss.

"Nico!" Laughing, James tried to peel the squirmy four-year-old off his back. "What are you doing?"

"Attack!" Gianni joined in, throwing his fifty pounds at James, too.

Kyra darted over from the sidelines to help. "It's James's turn to toss," she said, trying to get a hold of Nico. "Why would you attack him, boys?"

Nico was still clawing, both of them trying to get James down.

"He tell us to," Gianni said.

James sputtered and gave up the fight, letting the little guys take him down to the ground. "I did not," he denied hotly, or as hotly as a man could when he was being annihilated by tiny humans. Mostly, he was laughing.

Gianni held tight to James's sleeve. "You said 'attack the opponent.'"

"In business and Monopoly, little dude. Not a friendly game of bocce on a sunny afternoon."

Gianni gave a gap-toothed grin, hesitated a second,

then launched again. "Attack!" This time, James went down on his back, and Nico jumped up, hopping from one foot to the other in unadulterated delight.

"They attack because they love," Kyra assured him, placing a warm hand on his arm.

"Then why don't you?" he teased.

"Later." She gave him a secret wink. "Come on, boys. Nonna has cookies."

Gianni was off him in a second, bouncing to his feet and grabbing his brother's arm. Kicking dirt behind them, they took off, but James watched as they ran across the courtyard and into the kitchen.

"They love cookies more than me," he said.

"I don't." She leaned over and kissed him lightly. "I love you more than anything."

He threaded his hands into her hair. "Same, same, same." He met her lips again and enjoyed the sweet, heady sensation of kissing in the sun. "I love you so much."

"Enough to spend two months in Italy."

"Best two months of my life."

"James!" Filippa called from the tables where most of the family was still eating a long, late lunch, holding up a cell phone. "*Telefono!*"

"That's Finn," he said, standing and offering his hand. "We've been texting, and it's been a bear with the time difference. It's about five in the morning in Alaska now. C'mon. Let's tell him the news. Poor kid is the last one to know everything in this family."

"And the last one to deal with his legacy," Kyra reminded him as she brushed some dirt off her jeans.

James couldn't help smiling. "I really can't wait to see him go down."

"Go down?" She took his hand and walked toward

JAMES

Filippa, who still held the phone. "Maybe not the best thing to wish on a guy who inherited airplanes."

"True." He smiled at her and brought their joined hands to his lips. "But he can't break the streak. Brannigans are six for seven, and Finn may be last, but that guy is never least. Come on, we'll put him on speaker and officially introduce you two."

With a nod to Filippa, James took the phone and tapped the screen, draping an arm around Kyra and walking off the courtyard. "Hey, Finn, my young boy, how are you?"

"Not your young boy," he said with an easy laugh. "Any more than you are Perfect James."

"For once, that stupid nickname is correct." He beamed at Kyra, guiding her down a few stone stairs to a bench overlooking the vineyard. "I'm not perfect, but everything around me is *perfecto*."

Kyra laughed at his bad Italian accent, but Finn choked softly in surprise.

"Are you still in Italy?" Finn asked. "How long can it take to sell a winery?"

"Oh, the winery sold a long time ago, but I want you to say hello to Kyra Summers, who happens to be the love of my life and your next sister-in-law."

For a moment, Finn was dead silent, and Kyra and James shared a look.

"Hi, Finn," she said, biting her lip, her eyes dancing. "It's nice to phone-meet you."

"You, too, Kyra. Damn, James. You're getting married? Seems like I'm getting these kinds of calls from my brothers on a monthly basis."

James laughed. "Do you see a pattern here?"

"Not exactly. When's the big day?" Finn asked.

"We're headed back to New York tomorrow to get

Kyra set up with me, maybe find a nice place in Connecticut with a lot of land." He squeezed her hand and watched the slow smile deepen her dimples. A *lot* of land. And many rooms for a growing family.

"So, the wedding's in New York, then?" Finn asked. "When?"

"Actually," Kyra said, leaning closer to the phone. "We're getting married here in Positano in October, right after the harvest. We're having a great big Italian wedding, and we want all the Brannigan brothers here. I want to meet everyone."

Finn gave a hearty laugh. "And you'll never be the same, but I think I can swing that. I...think."

James could picture his little brother running his hand through his short, military cut, maybe rubbing a few-days-old whiskers he could grow on that big square jaw of his now that he was out of the Navy.

"So, what's going on up there in Alaska?" James asked. "Did you figure out a way to sell those planes like I suggested?"

"I gotta say, James, these are decent planes. Better than that. He left me a de Havilland Beaver, which just happens to be the most quintessential, legendary bush floatplane ever made, and two Cessnas that switch out between wheels and skis."

James threw a smile at Kyra and mouthed, "The man loves to fly."

Her eyes sparkled as Finn continued.

"Osprey Air's turned out to be a good business," he said. "And while landing on a glacier might not have the same rush as doing a controlled crash on an aircraft carrier, it brings its own challenges."

But James knew it wasn't the challenge of landing planes on glaciers that Dad had in mind when he left

JAMES

Osprey Air to his youngest son. And he couldn't wait to find out what was in store for his adrenaline junkie brother.

"Any women around in Alaska?" James asked.

Finn snorted. "Yes, there are women."

"Anyone in particular?"

"Nothing against all you lovebirds, but I have no plans to succumb to this particular family trend that started when Dad died. I intend to remain the last bachelor brother standing."

James just laughed.

"And what's so funny?"

"Nothing," James said. "Can't a man laugh? I'm happy. And I want you to be, too. I think Dad wanted us all to be happy."

"Then he pulled it off," Finn said. "I'm happy whenever I'm in the air, and the family group email has never been so chirpy with brothers who finally have their shit together. I guess we can thank the old man for that."

"We can thank the old man for a lot of things," James said, putting his arm firmly around one of them. "He definitely knew what he was doing when he gave me this winery."

"Which you sold," Finn noted. "Of course you do bow to the almighty dollar."

He and Kyra shared a look. "Truth be told, I sold it for that almighty dollar."

"Knew it."

"*One* of them. One single dollar, and to the family who should own it." And James never felt better about a business investment in his life.

"Hmmm." Finn gave a grunt. "You think that's why Dad gave it to you? To set the ownership straight?"

"No, Dad gave it to me so I could learn a simple lesson."

"Which is?" Finn asked.

James took a breath and hoped his Italian was spot-on. "*La famiglia è tutto.*"

Finn laughed at the incomprehensible words, but then his laughter faded. "Wait a second. I've seen that before."

"Amazed you remember it, Finn. It was on a little box Mom had and Dad kept around for a few years. It means..." James hesitated. "It means that you better be at our wedding, bro. You and whoever you want to bring."

"I'll be there alone," Finn assured him. "Keep me posted on the family email chain. I have a foursome of seniors waiting to check a flight over Denali off their bucket lists, so I have to go. Congrats again, brother. And welcome to the Brannigan clan, Kyra. Any woman who could convince James to stop working for two months must be incredible indeed."

"She is," James said.

They signed off, and James leaned back, nestling Kyra into his side, the two of them looking out over the endless, gorgeous expanse of the Amalfi Coast. "You know what, lemondrop?"

She sighed and put her head on his shoulder. "What?"

"I never thought I'd say this, but I hope I can be half the father my Ddad was."

"And I'll be twice the mother mine was." She gave him a nudge. "You didn't tell him *all* the news."

"It'll be pretty obvious by October." He looked down at her, gauging her expression. "Are you sure you don't want to rush the wedding and just have a party in October after the harvest?"

"I'm sure. You sure you want to go in there right now and tell the family?"

He brought her to a slow stand. "Yeah, because that'll be…fun."

She laughed. "They have themselves to blame. They need to know what happens when two people get 'cozy.'"

Kissing her on the head, he led her back up the stairs to the sounds of laughter and clanging dishes and a noisy, happy, large, and secure family. The sounds were as sweet as the grapes that grew around them, and the lifetime of love that lay ahead.

About the Author

Published since 2003, Roxanne St. Claire is a New York Times and USA Today bestselling author of more than forty romance and suspense novels. She has written several popular series, including Barefoot Bay, the Guardian Angelinos, and the Bullet Catchers.

In addition to being an eight-time nominee and one-time winner of the prestigious RITA™ Award for the best in romance writing, Roxanne's novels have won the National Reader's Choice Award for best romantic suspense three times, as well as the Maggie, the Daphne du Maurier Award, the HOLT Medallion, Booksellers Best, Book Buyers Best, the Award of Excellence, and many others.

She lives in Florida with her husband, and still attempts to run the lives of her teenage daughter and 20-something son. She loves dogs, books, chocolate, and wine, but not always in that order.

www.roxannestclaire.com
www.twitter.com/roxannestclaire
www.facebook.com/roxannestclaire

SIGN UP FOR HER NEWSLETTER AND RECEIVE
A FREE FULL LENGTH NOVEL!
www.roxannestclaire.com/newsletter/